HOMELAND
THE LAST GENERATION

Order this book online at www.trafford.com/0
or email orders@trafford.com

Most Trafford titles are also available at major online book retailers.

Note for Librarians: A cataloguing record for this book is available from Library
and Archives Canada at www.collectionscanada.ca/amicus/index-e.html

Printed in Victoria, BC, Canada.

ISBN: 978-1-4251-0920-2

*Our mission is to efficiently provide the world's finest, most comprehensive
book publishing service, enabling every author to experience success.
To find out how to publish your book, your way, and have it available
worldwide, visit us online at www.trafford.com/*

Trafford rev. 10/29/09

www.trafford.com

North America & international
toll-free: 1 888 232 4444 (USA & Canada)
phone: 250 383 6864 ♦ fax: 812 355 4082

DEDICATION

I dedicate this book to my Lord and Savior Jesus Christ. Without His vision and anointing this book would not have been made possible. Also, to the wonderful family God has graciously allowed me to share here on this earth. To David, my husband, who is a wonderful man who walks with God. For that reason he has shown me nothing but love and respect. I am so grateful that God gave me the wonderment of his love here on earth.

To my two children who have honoured me with more love and pride than any one mother deserves. They have looked Satan in the eye and have earned the right to be individuals in this world to walk with God's grace. Candy and Billy have brought me much joy in my life. I pray God will continue to show them His grace.

Also, to my grandson Tripp, who knows how much joy he has brought to my life. He too believes that promises should not be broken and that God loves him and that our Savior Jesus Christ will never leave him or for-sake him. "Oh no Tripp I love you more!"

To Patrice and Phil Humphries, the dear Christian family and friends who have walked with me, cried with me, mourned with me, and laughed and prayed with me. To my loving friends that I have been able to share my ministry with to help change lives and give hope back to the forgotten in our world.

I would also like to thank my loving shepherd and his angel, Rev. Bill & Ollie Jolly. Rev. Jolly guarded one of his sheep and led her in the right direction to the purpose of her life. May God keep you and your angel safe within His caring arms.

ACKNOWLEDGEMENTS

As always, a novel like Word Walkers does not come together without the hard work of more than just one person. I would like to thank my family for trusting the vision that God gave me, when I had no other choice but do as I felt was the anointing of this book to be written and given to the generations of the world. Many times I have had to ask help from my family. On more than one occasion they have taken precious time of their own to see that the book publishing process went as smoothly as possible.

I want to thank my new friends at Trafford Publishing. Thank you for your hard work and dedication in the publication of this book. I'd like to give a special thanks to my Publishing Consultants, Carmen Dunn and Elaine Shoemaker. Your kindness in helping me see my vision for this series and my place as a Best Selling Author came straight from your expert opinions. Your encouragement and excitement gave me a visual of the true heart of the book that I never envisioned before. I also want to thank all those that put long hours into making the Word Walker Series come alive.

I also want to thank Patrice Humphries and Hollie Pittman for their loving friendship which engulfed me and my implanted vision from God on the importance of this book getting into the hands of our last generation. Their long hours of editing and prayers over presentation and future marketing planning has assured the success in the blueprint that God had intended for this series to make a defendant impact in the lives of all that read this book.

A NEW BEGINNING FOR ALL OF US

Love I hope and pray I have shown and engraved in the hearts of the precious lives God allowed me to care for here on earth. To them I pray God's blessings and fruitfulness as long as the Love of life is within them. For without this Love their lives are doomed to a never ending living death. I pray I have not failed them. If in some way I have, I ask for their and God's forgiveness.

I can promise you this. Here in America we will become a nation where the majority will live without God as a presence in its people's lives. Yes, we were once a nation that surrounded ourselves with the rights of a Nation who trusted its generations of new lives to God, but no more. We have blocked God out of the hearts of a whole generation of children. *This is our lost generation.* Let us not forget the generation we murdered and are still murdering today, *the unborn.*

We should as American Christians embrace this generation and hold it close to our hearts or we will lose it too. *This will be our last generation.* Wouldn't it be great if we could do a little damage control?

What? Didn't you know we have already lost one generation? What in the name of our Savior, Jesus can we as Christians do to lead the lost and grab hold of the ones who have fallen away? We need the help of a Christian nation to bring the lost generation in to the flock. All we have left are the little ones, the children. Trying to make a whole world notice will take the life out of them and they will not stay children long. It looks like the path to our salvation will be led by our children.

You say, "Well of course it will. It always has been."

Yes, you are correct, although this time it will be different.

Once, America was a great nation and as far as most of the world sees us we still are. America still needs to embrace its people as a nation. We all wonder what has happened to our children. The answer to that is in asking the right question. *"Where are the parents?"*

I QUOTE YOU A POEM FROM
TIMELESS VOICES, JUST RE-
LEASED AUGUST 2006 BY THE
INTERNATIONAL LIBRARY OF
POETRY.

WHERE TO START

The questions of a child
In this day of crime
Are as strong as the passing of time
With a tear in his eye and a pain in his heart
Where, where to start?
In this day and time
When he asks the why of the crime,
Where are the parents
To answer the fear in this child's heart?
Where, where to start?
If Dad and Mom would go back to the cross,
Do you think that there it could start?
At the foot of the cross,
And in Dad's and Mom's hearts?

WRITTEN BY

Audrey Hines

THE WORD

I JOHN 1: 5-7

5- This then is the message which we have heard of him, and declare unto you, that God is light, and in him is no darkness at all.

6- If we say that we have fellowship with him, and walk in darkness, we lie, and do not the truth:

7- But if we walk in the light, as he is in the light, we have fellowship one with another, and the blood of Jesus Christ his Son cleanseth us from all sin.

ST. JOHN 1: 14

14-And the Word was made flesh, and dwelt among us, (and we beheld his glory, the glory as of the only begotten of the Father,) full of grace and truth.

THE WALKER

ROMANS 14: 8

8- For whether we live, we live unto the Lord; and whether we die, we die unto the Lord: whether we live therefore, or die, we are the Lord's.

I JOHN 2: 4-6

4- He that saith, I know him, and keepeth not his commandments, is a liar, and the truth is not in him.

5- But whoso keepeth this word in him verily (truly) is the love of God perfected: herby Know (realize) we that we are in him

6- He that saith he abideth (lives) in him ought himself also so to walk, even as he walked.

PROPHECY

KING JAMES VERSION

I JOHN: 2: 18, 28-29

18- Little children, it is the last time: and as ye have heard that antichrist shall come, even now are there many antichrists; whereby we know (realize) that it is the last time.

28- And now, little children, abide in him; that, when he shall appear, we may have confidence (boldness), and not be ashamed (embarrassed), at his coming.

29- If ye know that he is righteous, ye know that every one that doth righteousness is born of him.

LUKE 21: 31-33

31- So likewise ye, when ye see these things come (happen) of your own selves that summer is now nigh at hand.

32- Verily (truly) I say unto you, this generation shall not pass away, till all be fulfilled.

33- Heaven and earth shall pass away: but my words shall not pass away.

ISAIAH 8: 18

18- Behold, I and the children whom the Lord hath given me are for signs and for wonders in Israel from the Lord of hosts, which dwelleth in mount Zion.

ROMANS 11:25-26

25- For I would not, brethren, that ye should be ignorant of this mystery, lest ye should be wise in your own conceits (proud ideas); that blindness (hardness) in part is happened to Israel, until the fullness of the Gentiles be come in.

26- And so all Israel shall be saved: as it is written, there shall come out of Zion the Deliverer, and shall turn away ungodliness from Jacob (the children of God).

PROPHECY

KING JAMES VERSION

ACTS 3: 19-26

19- Repent ye therefore, and be converted, that your sins may be blotted out, when the times of refreshing shall come from the presence of the Lord:

20- And he shall send Jesus Christ, which before was preached unto you:

21- Whom the heaven must receive until the times of restitution of all things, which God hath spoken by the mouth of all his holy prophets since the world began.

22- For Moses truly said unto the fathers, A prophet shall the Lord your God raise up unto you of your brethren, like unto me; him shall ye hear in all things whatsoever he shall say unto you.

23- And it shall come to pass, that every soul, which will not hear that prophet, shall be destroyed from among the people.

24- Yea, and all the prophets from Samuel and those that follow after, as many as have spoken, have like wise foretold of these days.

25- Ye are the children of the prophets, and of the covenant which God make with our fathers, saying unto Abraham, and in thy (your) seed shall all the kindred's of the earth be blessed.

26- Unto you first God, having raised up his Son Jesus, (his servant) sent him to bless you, in turning away every one of you from his iniquities (turning everyone from their sin).

CHAPTER ONE

MAGNA

During the latter part of the twenty-first century the world as we knew it had rapidly changed. Terrorism was worse than ever. There were actual civil wars within individual countries. Starvation was rampant in all nations. Even in America disease, hunger, fighting, and killing were a way of life. The government in America had turned away from the Constitution of the old United States. For some of us, we had no other choice but to take a stand to protect the parts of our human souls from being destroyed, and to protect the only thing that made us a human race. There were not many of us left, but we soon found out that there would be enough to carry on the Word of our Lord and Savior Jesus Christ.

Although we were scattered around the world God would see to it that we had the knowledge of how to find each other when we were needed. He will make sure to remind us all that no matter how bad the condition of the world becomes, our Lord Jesus is with us all to the end. Sacrifices will be made by all of us. That is what our story is all about.

As I try to look back to where the turning point of my old life ended and my new life started, my first memories begin with the early morning sun in my face and the winter's cold winds blowing my hair in the wet breeze of the sea. The Straut family, my family of four, were on our knees in the soft, cold, damp, sandy beach off a small western coast line of the northern part of the state of Washington. This sandy beach we so humbly knelt upon was part of a small fishing and tourist town called Three Ridges. People used to come here a lot, all year long. Vacationing was wild and wonderful for all of us town folk and tourist alike.

Spring, summer, fall, or winter, it didn't matter what the season, Three Ridges was always ready for tourists to pay us a visit, or at least it used to be. That had changed too. It was hard for people to travel from town to town anymore. Government laws forbid people from crossing county and state lines without being checked out first. If you tried to cross barrier lines without permission you could be arrested or even killed. Gas had to be rationed so there were no airplanes allowed to fly civilians, everyone travelled by bus, motor bikes, and by foot. You had to take turns crossing the lines after you had proven there was no concern to worry about you and your companions that wanted entry into the next county. Not only that, all goods of food or any other articles that the government didn't think you needed to cross the line with were confiscated, and you were rationed on items from gas to ice and everything in between.

The sun rose early on this very unusual morning and so did we. I didn't mind getting up early but I didn't understand why we had to come down to the beach before breakfast. Something was wrong. I, now only twelve years of age, was doing all I could just to do as I was told, yet still this morning everything was strange and somehow very different.

Everyone was so quiet. The first words I can re-call were the words of prayer coming from Father. I wanted to say something but I knew not to interrupt when Father was praying. No matter what was going on around you there was one thing you didn't question. While in prayer you let matters of the world handle themselves.

Father was a big man and usually extremely healthy. Today, however, as I looked up at him as he prayed, I noticed a difference in him. As his sandy brown hair moved with the wind I could see a little grey within the thick cut of his hair line. Father's face once was young and strong. Now, however, it had a strange look about it. He looked tired and old. As the words of Father's prayer grew silent to my ears, I began looking close into the faces of the rest of my family.

Mother's beautiful long blonde hair was also blow-ing in the wind. Mother was the one who always had a smile on her face, but not today. Tears were running gently from her eyes, drying salty and sticky on her face. As she held my hand I could feel her trembling.

Fear began to swell up inside of me. I was almost afraid to continue with my circular inspection of my family. I finally found the courage to move along to my brother, Evan. As I did, our eyes met. It startled me at first, for I knew we were supposed to be praying.

Evan was also especially strongly built for a fourteen year old. He reminded me a lot of Father. Every one of our friends was always saying, "You could pick Ethan Straut's son out of a crowd. They are just alike, you're your father's son all right, Evan."

Somehow today Evan, too, was different. As I looked closer into Evan's eyes I realized that indeed something was very wrong. Very, very wrong! His face was so sad. Taking a closer look into his eyes was where I learned the truth. Evan knew something horrible that I didn't know. As our eyes gazed deeper into each others souls, Evan clenched my hand tighter and tighter. You see, Evan and I had a secret, one that only he and I knew about. Besides, in the world we lived in, if you weren't close to family, you weren't close to anyone. So depending on each other for our very lives did bond us a little closer to one another than most brothers and sisters. I somehow knew he wished within his heart that he would never have to let go. It was as if I knew my brother's every thought. I could hear my soul's voice ever so softly within me.

"Magna, little Magna who will watch after you now?"

I shuddered within. What did my soul mean? Evan would of course take care of me. He was always there if I needed a stronger nudge to keep me safe from the other kids at school or if I didn't quite get all my homework done, and always there when I strayed too far out on the cliffs. What did my soul mean? It didn't take long for me to realize that these were very small matters that would never matter again.

All of a sudden Father's voice broke the stillness. "Amen."

Evan and I both turned toward Father as our prayer to our loving Lord ended. We stood up in silence. With the wind blowing in our faces we dropped hands, separating ourselves, like robots programmed to do it just the right way.

There was a tiny boat that was waiting to the side of us, half way in the sea and half on the beach. It scared me to look at it as it sat there brushing in time with the tide. As I continued to look at it I remember thinking, "We weren't going anywhere in that tiny nip of a boat, especially this time of the year?" Mother had just gotten it for her thirty-fifth birthday. Surely Mother had not learned to sail that well yet. Well, I really didn't know what to think. I really didn't know what was going on.

Evan looked at me once more, for only a second. He then turned his face quickly from me and walked over to hold the boat more securely in place. Meanwhile, Father quietly moved Mother and me to the side of the boat. With tears and soft words of love my father told my mother how much he loved her. Not only with his words, but you could also tell his heart was breaking as he unwillingly picked her up and placed her safely in the boat.

It was not hard for Father to snatch Mother up, for she was a tiny woman. It was the look in both their eyes that astounded me. It was Father's face that sadness consumed. For to hold her, kiss her, or look upon her beauty was the one thing that Father loved to do. This time the sorrow in his face somehow let me know he felt like it was for the last time. I don't know how I knew but I knew none the less. Surely my soul was wrong this time?

As unwillingly as my father placed my mother in the tiny boat, he unwillingly but obediently let her go. With one last glimpse of her he turned his attention toward me. Father grabbed me, holding me tight to his chest. He kissed my face all over, laughing only a little, and then placed me by my mother's side in the boat. He pulled me close to the edge, looking at every inch of my face. He gently pulled a long strand of my hair out of my face and told me how beautiful I was and how glad he was I took after my mother. I watched him ever so closely as he spoke to me. I was enjoying his smile and his soft words until suddenly the fear in his heart overwhelmed his face once more. His fear became mine and I'm glad it did, for it gave me the courage to finally speak as I saw him start to turn to walk away.

Grabbing his arm and pulling him back I shouted, "Father! Why can't you and Evan come with Mother and me? You're not staying here without us are you?"

I could tell by the sadness in his face and how he avoided looking me in the eye that that was just what he had planned.

"Why do we have to go away without you? Can't we stay together?"

As I spoke his eyes became gentle again. Where once a fearful face consumed him, love, peace, and a wide smile came into view once more. Father looked me straight in the eyes and said,

"Oh Magna, your mother and I knew that this day would one day come. We have prepared for this day in our family for generations. Our family saw this day coming in the word of God a long, long time ago. The final beginning to the coming of our Savior is almost upon us. We must now prepare ourselves. The world will only get worse after our Christ comes for his children. Until that time, the world needs us to gather as many souls as we can now. As the Word of God states:

> *For in those days shall be affliction, such as was not from the beginning of the creation which God created unto this time, neither shall be. And except that the Lord had shortened those days, no flesh should be saved: but for the elect's sake, whom he hath chosen, he hath shortened the days. And then if any man shall say to you, Lo, here is Christ: or, lo, he is there; believe him not: For false Christ and false prophets shall rise, and shall shew signs and wonders, to seduce, if it were possible, even the elect.* Mark 13:19-23."

Father continued, "You see Magna, our world is racing to catch up with that scripture. The world that you know is about to change into something even worse than it is now. It has already started. Our world here is not safe for you and Mother anymore. I must send you to a much safer place than this. We must all start to prepare for the second coming of our Lord Jesus. Evan must stay here with me so that I can prepare him for what is about to happen to our world as we know it now. You, my little Magna, must go with your mother so that she can prepare you. I don't know how long you will have to stay away, but you will come back some-day ready to do your part to help prepare for His com-ing. Now, you stop worrying about everything. You and Mother are going to be just fine."

As he was talking to me he motioned for Evan to push the boat into the sea. Evan obeyed Father just as he always had.

"No, Father! Don't send us away!" I screamed and grabbed for him. I tried to hold on to him but he made me let him go. The foamy grey waves bounded as the tide took me and Mother further and further away from the beach. I was crying so hard, I don't know how, but somehow over the waves of the sea and my screams I could hear Father's voice loud and strong.

"Remember, my little Magna, listen and learn ev-erything your mother tells you."

"No! I don't want to! Not without you and Evan!"

"We have been chosen. Our lives are not our own. They belong to God. Be strong. Have courage!"

Mother now had a tight grip on me, for I was trying to jump out of the tiny vessel that was taking me away from the other half of my life that I loved.

"I don't want to be strong! Father don't, don't let us go!"

"Never, ever forget the word of our Savior. Prepare, make yourself worthy my little Magna!"

As the sound of the sea overpowered my father's voice the last thing I heard him say was, "Remember! To live is to die! Remember! Remember!"

As Father's voice faded over the sound of the sea mother brought me close to her. I remember the waves of the sea taking us further and further away until we could no longer see the shore line, Father, or Evan. They were gone.

I sadly looked up at my mother and was shocked to see that her tears were gone. The fear in her face had disappeared. Without speaking a word to one another we looked at each other and smiled. In my heart I knew Mother and I were thinking the same thing. We would remember. No matter what we would never forget Father's last words to us. To live is to die! I didn't know what these unusual words meant or what meaning they would bring to our lives but I knew they must have meant everything to Father. It had some kind of deep abounding love that I didn't understand.

I knew with all my heart that someday God would let me know. I found the courage to straighten my shoulders and stand in a very proud manner by my mother's side. I was determined that no matter what, I would never forget. Yes, I would be ready and waiting for God to show me the meaning of, "*To live is to die.*"

CHAPTER TWO

EVAN

I stood by my Father's side as I watched the sea take my mother and sister away. I could hear my heart beat within my chest as time stood still around me. Time standing still, yet passing so quickly. I felt as if I would never see Mother or Magna again. Little did I realize just how close my heart was to the truth.

Mother was the one who had always been my watchful eye to show me the softness and kindness of the world. She always seemed to make all the problems in my world just melt away with her laughter and smiles. Mother could always draw a picture of goodness from anything I thought was the worst thing in life that could ever happen to me.

Magna was my wonderment in life. She was good and kind like Mother, but seemed to always be getting into things she was not supposed to. Magna was always drawn to places, people, and certain creatures that put her in the wrong place at the wrong time. Like all big brothers, I was always there to get her out of trouble and back on track. It also made me very nervous for her. Without me around, who would pull her out of the other half of the world that would draw her so harshly into itself? This may sound strange to you but in a brotherly kind of way I was going to miss that. I know it's silly but I loved my sister very much. Magna had a spiritual gift that God blessed her with. I was the only other one that knew about it. It was our secret. I was always making sure she kept herself safe and out of harm's way.

This secret drew us closer than most brothers and sisters. I've always been there to keep her in check of her spiritual talent from God. We never let mother and father know anything about it. I'm sure they would have forbidden her from doing such dangerous things. Our closeness also came from the fact that the world had changed so much, that family was sometimes the only friend you had during the good and bad times.

I was now realizing that the waves were taking them farther and farther from my life forever. I was feeling as if all the good and tender things of my life were floating away with them. All my love was pouring out of my heart like the sands of an hour glass. Lost forever, or so it felt like it anyway. I, unlike Magna, had been a part of this world long enough to know the breaking of the heart and what it could do to people. I had seen it many times when I went to the city with Father. Families' hopes and dreams gone forever. All the homeless, hungry, and forgotten people with their faces filled with blank emotions are so horrible! Oh, I didn't even want to think about it anymore. After all, the world couldn't get much worse, and besides, we weren't like those people.

I tried to be as brave as I knew Mother would want me to be. I was so desperately trying to find the faith that I needed to instill courage within me. I could hear Mother's voice ringing inside my ear.

"The sea is big, but certainly not as big as God. There is a reason, Son, I promise. All you need to do is just hold on to your faith."

I was trying, but between the faith and the pain the pain beneath my chest swelled up inside of me like someone was blowing up a balloon. The pain was becoming more overwhelming and I could no longer look at the emptiness of the sea. Mother and Magna were well on their way now. I could no longer see the tiny boat or their faces anymore. They were gone.

My father stood with me watching my mother and sister drift away. His silence was what assured me of how alone I truly felt. Not able to look into the vast, cold, and now empty ocean any longer, my father watched without any words as I turned and walked towards the rocks of the shoreline. You could tell in his face he knew I had more questions than he could answer. He just had that look about him. You know the one, concerned, but blank.

My Father knew my faith in God was young and maybe had not matured enough to bear too many more losses too quickly. He knew my spirit was breaking as he stood over me for a long time in silence, as I just sat there looking into the sand. He finally sat down beside me. He sat close to me, but the silence was still empowering him. The silence was scaring the life out of me. I had to do something, say something, anything, but I could no longer deal with his silence. I finally found the courage to speak. I could no longer be obedient in this silence any longer!

"Father, why is God doing this to us? Why must it be us that have to give up all and each other? This is not right, Father, this is just not right!"

Father put his arm around my shoulders. He was trying to show me his love and I could also tell he was trying to show me respect. I didn't question the respect but I did question his love. Respect he had always shown me, although this did seem different. I was trying to be understanding but how could he? How could he do this? How could a man love his family and just give them up to be swallowed up in the world without anyone to take care of them? My anger was engulfing my soul and I didn't know how to handle it. I don't think I have ever been angry in my life. I kept looking up at Father for a quick answer. The more I waited, the angrier I became. I finally came to the conclusion that these were going to be the questions I would never get answered. I also came to the final conclusion that I at least deserved something to explain this madness.

Still looking up at Father, watching his every move, I could tell he was searching for something to say. Father always got that faithful look on his face when he was searching for just the right words. You know the look I'm talking about. The one where he really doesn't know the answer but he is sure his heart and his faith will come up with just what God would want him to say. If you have been raised by or around people of great religious faith, then you know what I'm talking about. It has to do with the renewing of the mind or something like that. You know, what would Jesus do? Or how would God explain this since I'm only human. I waited in the silence, which seemed to take forever. Half the day was already gone when, like a soft burst of wind, Father spoke.

"Evan."

It took my breath when the quietness was shattered. After the sudden shock I began to pray.

"God, please let Father tell me something that would take this pain away. Please, Lord, please!"

"Evan, my son, God is not punishing us. He is blessing us. You see, Evan, our Lord and Savior Jesus left his family to go out into the world to prepare them. He taught his Word to all who would listen. He gave himself as the Lamb to be sacrificed for our sins. He died a horrible death on the cross. But that is not where it ended. He arose again, on the third day, Son, to assure us eternal life. Evan, you know this about your Savior. Your mother and I have taught you this all your life. He did this willingly.

"Son, He died because he loved us. He arose to give us life. The one thing that all Christians soon find out is that sooner or later there will be a time in their lives when they will be glad to give up all they think they have to conserve the Word of our Lord Jesus Christ. You think you are giving up everything that is important to you, Son, but you have already given everything you own to the Lord, including your soul. Now that your soul belongs to God you can't have it back!"

"I'm not asking anything back from God, that is wrong! I just don't understand why it has to be us."

"Evan, you can't say that even you haven't seen our world around us change. You of all people have seen how our small town has changed just in the last few years. You have been working with me in the city. I know that you have seen the pain and suffering in those people's lives. Son, it is not going to get better for them or us, it is only going to get worse. Most of the signs of our Lord's coming have plainly already come to pass; now all the other governments around the world are taking the New Testament from all the Christian religious based nations of the world where it is taught. We Christians can't let this happen."

"I understand that we are different from the world. You have always taught us that. But why does all the sacrificing have to start with us!"

"You have seen the ungodly terror in our world today. Our world has decreased in its moral and spiritual beliefs. Just because the inter-global countries of the world want world peace, they think taking the New Testament out of the world and hiding it from the eyes and ears of the world is going to stop the hate in people's hearts for each other and save the people in this world.

"God's people have been blinded by the material possessions in this world that the government is promising to give them. They are also blinded by the fact that most people believe in a higher Godhead. Most people believe in God, or at least some kind of God. The horrible reality, Son, is that not everyone believes in Jesus, The Lord and Savior of the world! Our government is taking the Word of Christ away from us, and there is a law right now in Congress that will not allow the New Testament or our Savior's name to even be spoken about in any manner. This is not only going on in our country, but in all nations around the world. We have to stand and fight for the time needed to lead the lost to Christ."

"Father, you act like I've never heard you preach! I know what the Word says about what Christ did for us, but a loving God doesn't do this to His people. How can we stand up to the whole world?"

"You see, Son, the government leaderships of the world feel that since all people believe in God, that all people can get along. If they can unite worldwide there will be no more Holy wars with nation against nation. It is Jesus that the majority of the international countries have a problem with. For many years there was a great revival across the world and things seemed to be going good for most, although while everything looked good, the world itself just kept right on spiralling more and more out of control. We are in the end times. You, my son, and the children in this world just may be the last generation. The world will never be able to come to a one world government with total peace without removing the New Testament. This, Son, is just the beginning of the trade off. This trade off is souls for power. This trade off is one that the Christians can't afford to accept. There are thousands of true Christians now, but to remove the New Testament from people's hearts on a daily basis will only allow them to stray away from righteous living. Not only that Son, how will the lost come to know their last hope for eternal salvation?"

Sobbing and wiping my eyes on the back of my hand, I managed to blubber something out like, "We can't save a whole world!"

"It is not our place to save the world. It is our place to lead the world to Jesus, one soul at a time. This is called The Great Commission. The world today is just like when God's people were under bondage in Sodom. Sodom, as you know, was so bad and filled with every ungodly sin imaginable to man that God had to destroy it.

"God's people are also under bondage like they were when they were in Egypt. When the Israelites were in bondage they were God's own people, but everyday they woke up and lived by the commands of a worldly king's instruction instead of their Heavenly God. They tried to follow the laws lovingly passed down by their parents, but, just as in our world today, most of the world would rather do as the world instead of following all the Laws of God. You see, Evan, they believed in God as a mighty God, but they did not know him. To know about something and to actually believe in what you know are two different ways of thinking. One way is with the head and the other is with the heart.

"More so than these, the world will come to be as in the time of Noah. The second coming of Christ is at hand and He will come in the twinkling of an eye. It has already started. The people of this world and the world as Christians know it is going to come to a horrible end. More and more, true love is taken out of our lives and hearts every day. A world without love, and I mean the knowledge of and the acceptance of the true knowledge of our Lord Jesus Christ, is truly a condemned and totally doomed world.

"When our Savior Jesus comes back for his children, it will surely be a wondrous time, but you see, Son, our family will be okay. We have accepted the Lord Jesus as our Savior. We know how much He loves us. We are saved from the horrible end, but what about the others to come? What about the people out there right now, Son? What about those who don't have a clue who Jesus is? A world without the knowledge of true Love, as I said, Son, is doomed forever. Unless some of us take a stand to preserve the Word, the Wisdom, the Hope, and the Love left to us by our Lord and Savior Jesus Christ, there will only be one last chance of hope for those who have not accepted Jesus already. This hope lies after the rapture of the church, in the coming of an angel having the everlasting gospel who will preach unto those left behind dwelling on earth to every nation, kindred, tongue and people, shouting, 'Fear God and give glory to him. The time of judgment is come.' He demands that all will worship the Lord thy God; in the heaven and earth and all things in it. Revelation 14: 6-7.

"I hope you understand, Son. We have no other choices left. I know that you feel that all your joy, love, and hope just floated away forever, but that is not the truth my son. You must believe this. Romans 15:13 says, 'May the God of hope fill you with all joy and peace as you trust in Him, so that you may overflow with hope…'"

"But why does it have to be us? Why!"

"You know I choose the way of our Lord, Evan. I am a missionary of the Gospel of our Holy Savior. I know that it seems that our family is being split apart right now but we must be strong and trust in our Savior, Jesus."

As I sat there looking at Father as he spoke, I was totally confused. I knew Father had something to tell me with all those words but the pain in my heart was only getting worse. The pain was turning into anger. Really bad anger! I jumped up to my feet, knocking my foot upon the sand, and yelled with the sound of thunder.

"But Father, why does it have to be us? This is too much to ask from anyone! What about all this letting us choose our way? Huh? What about it Father?"

Father was shocked at my anger. He had never seen this side of me before. The reason for that is because I had never felt this way before. He sat there looking straight into my eyes. He knew that my heart was indeed breaking, if not already broken. At first Father didn't know what to say. Instead he took his finger and said,

"Look, Evan."

I stood there and watched him write in the sand. As the letters came together I read these words, "Jesus Wept." Father, with as compassionate a voice as possible, began to speak again.

"Son, indeed today our hearts are broken. That is why we cannot let the words of our Christ be thrown away, never to be heard again. For only Jesus can mend a broken heart. You see, Son, it's okay to cry. Jesus himself cried for the whole world.

"Psalm 34:17 - The righteous cry, and the Lord heareth, and deliverth them out of all their troubles.

"Isaiah 61:1-3 - The spirit of the Lord God is upon me; because the Lord hath anointed me to preach good tidings unto the meek; he hath sent me to bind up the broken hearted, to proclaim liberty to the captives, and the opening of the prison to them that are bound; to proclaim the acceptable year of the Lord, and the day of vengeance of our God; to comfort all that mourn. To appoint [assign] unto them that mourn in Zion, to give unto them beauty for ashes, the oil of joy for mourning, the garment of praise for the spirit of heaviness; that they might be called trees of righteousness, the planting of the Lord, that he might be glorified."

Looking at the words in the sand, "Jesus wept," and wanting desperately to feel something besides this pain, I just couldn't be strong any longer as my heart felt as if it would burst. My body fell limp onto my knees. Trying to hold the rest of my body up became impossible. My body became so heavy I couldn't hold it up any longer. I just fell onto the sands beneath me. There my tears poured out onto the sand for what seemed to be hours.

Father started to pray. Psalm 34:18 - "The Lord is nigh [near] unto them that are of a broken heart; and saveth such as be of a contrite [crushed] spirit."

I'm sure he didn't realize the pain this was going to put his family through. I image he just assumed that our faith was as strong as his. He clearly knew now that only Jesus would be able to heal my heart. Our Savior's promise was all he had left to hold on to when it came to me. If his son could not take his destiny now, maybe one day he would return to the love which now seemed to be stolen from him so suddenly and harshly.

With my wailing and crying, and Father, with his arms stretched out toward heaven and his voice shouting prayer unto his Lord and Savior, with the winds crashing the waves of the ocean against the farthest rocks of the shore line, everything seemed loud, almost too loud. Then suddenly something happened. At the same time, Father and I noticed an unearthly silence accompanied with the same unearthly stillness. Even the sea seemed as if it had stopped. Father and I slowly looked around. We cautiously stood to our feet and we both looked up to the sky at the same time. We both felt a strange thickness in the air. It seemed as though the wind had stopped. The movement of clouds above us were standing still. Right there with all the silence surrounding us like a captive wall, we stood there looking face to face at each other. After a few minutes I found the courage to speak.

"Father, it's time for us to go home."

My father, now looking very old and tired, rounded an enlightened look into the eyes of his son. He saw his son go to his knees a young and innocent youth. The eyes he was looking into now belonged to a boy taking his first steps into manhood. A good man or a bad man,

Father knew in his heart that he did not know. He did know his son was no longer the son he had as this horrible day started. I watched Father's eyes fill with tears and then he tried to speak. As I continued to look into his worn face, he finally managed to utter words from beneath the tears.

"Yes, Son, we will need our rest. There will be hard times ahead."

Together we started up the rocky pathway, back up to the sandy beach cliffs where the house was. Each of us knowing that we were starting the new beginning of our own new destinies; each to his own. How to begin? Where and when it would end? I guess only our own hearts knew the answers to these questions. Or would we ever know the answers to this madness? I guess each day will take care of itself. As I continued to walk up the pathway to the house the only thing I can recall is telling God, from the bottom of my heart,

"Well, God, it's your turn now."

CHAPTER THREE

MAGNA

The first day of our journey upon the sea was very long and hot. Mother took control of the tiny boat with its small sail and fixed it with a stern hand in the direction in which she wanted it to go. Mother seemed to have everything outlined in her mind as to where and what she wanted the vessel to do for her. Working with the very small boat kept her pretty busy, but all the while you could hear her softly humming songs about our Lord. "Amazing Grace," When the Role is Called up Yonder," the old hymns were always Mother's favorites. However, she would still look around at me with her ever so sweet and watchful eye. You could tell her slight glimpses were of concern.

Besides the sweet humming coming from Mother the only other sounds were the wind flipping the sails and the roar of the waves of the sea as they bounced on the tiny vessel we were anchored in. Although we were in sight of land we were far enough out into the open sea that the seagull's cries could no longer be heard. I can say I had a little concern myself at the power of the waves as they bounded against the tiny vessel. Mother and I had never been so far out into the open sea alone.

This concerned me a lot but I had a lot of faith in Mother. Mother was always in control of herself. And I know without a shadow of a doubt that she would die before she would let anything happen to me.

Mother and I did not speak to one another all day. As night came upon us the silence was broken. Mother called my name,

"Magna!"

I turned sharply to find Mother looking down at me with that calming smile of hers. I replied right off.

"Yes Mother!"

"Magna, it's time for us to eat and then we will settle down for the night. After we eat you will need to get some sleep. I'm going to tie the sail down and you open the box there with our supplies. Be careful and move steady as not to stumble and fall."

As Mother went about with the sail I shuffled around until I got a firm grip on the supply box. The box was not very big. I found it to be very heavy and the lid was closed real tight. I suppose Mother wanted it as water proof as possible. It was a gripping experience but I finally got the lid off of the supplies.

Just as soon as I got the box open Mother was joining me in the bottom of the boat. Looking into the box, to my surprise, there was not a lot of food among the supplies. Then I noticed there were only two large jars of fresh drinking water. Just as Mother was getting a good steady seat she noticed the surprise in my face and, as always, Mother knew just what to say to put my heart at ease.

"Magna, now, would you just look at your face. God will supply all our needs. There is more than enough. We will have to be just a little careful and not eat everything all in one day."

Mother began to prepare us a small supper of cheese and bread. We also would share one glass of water between us. Mother bowed her head and began to pray,

"We want to thank you, Lord, for our food and for keeping us safe on our journey. Please, Father God, keep Evan and his Father safe and strong so that they can walk close to your most wondrous strength, the strength that only you can give them. We ask you, Lord, for the strength for us as a family to accept your will in our lives and to forgive us of our doubts of your will in our lives. May we show ourselves worthy to do your bidding as we continue to walk according to your word."

As the end of the prayer came with a very soft and humble, "Amen", we started to eat.

We still did not talk all through our meal. As our meal for the day came to an end Mother reached down and started to put the supply box back in its place, when I jumped in to help.

"I'll do it."

"Why thank you, Magna. If you will do this I will check to see that the sail and the boat are secure for the night." There was still great sadness in her voice.

With me helping, Mother finally got settled for the long night ahead. It didn't take Mother long to cuddle herself back by my side. She began to arrange me just like she wanted me in the bottom of the boat, placing one blanket under my head and carefully tucking the other around me. While all this fixing was taking place Mother kept asking,

"Are you sure you're comfortable down there?"

The bottom of the boat was a little hard but I returned my answer to Mother with a half cheerful, "I'm fine!"

As Mother sat beside me, she was now looking very tired. With a slight release of breath she adjusted herself. I watched her for a while. She pulled her hair back in a ponytail, wrapped a blanket around her shoulders, and leaned back to a smiling gaze at the stars.

They were so beautiful. I don't think I had ever noticed the stars being so big and bright before. They looked liked Christmas lights hanging all in just the right place against a giant, black velvet cloth. The stars and the darkness went on forever. That seemed strange to me since there wasn't a cloud in the sky anywhere. The waves were moving the boat around like a stick. Oh, I didn't want to think about that right now. Gazing into heaven like this made me a little less afraid of the vast ocean which we were now at odds with.

We both were very quiet for the longest time when suddenly a huge wave pounced on the tiny boat. It hit us so hard it threw my head off my pillow. This really got Mother's attention. As I came off the pillow I screamed as I reached up, throwing my arms around Mother's neck.

"Mother, I'm afraid!"

I had not really known just how afraid until I said it. Mother smiled and began to rub my face.

"Magna, my little Magna. Your life is not one to fear but one to be happy for. Oh, for you and our family the Day of Atonement is at hand. Lay your head back down and I will tell you a wonderful story. This is a story about what to expect of your new home."

Mother, giving me a little shove backward on my pillowed bed and assuring herself that I was just the way she wanted me for the night, began.

"Magna, you and I are on our way to a beautiful and most wondrous place. I don't want you to be afraid for where we are going there is nothing to be afraid of. There are other people just like you and me who are also on their way there right now. Like us, they are loving and courageous Christians chosen by God to save the Holy Word of our Lord and Savior Jesus Christ. Oh Magna, you will love your new home! It is where your Father and I were raised as children. We grew up together in the same township. I think I fell in love with your Father the first time I saw him fall into the creek that runs on the outlining edge of the sea river. I was only twelve years old."

Mother stopped and looked up into the stars for a moment or two. She was thinking of only Father now. I could tell, for her smile melted away and tears puddled in her eyes. Then all of a sudden she looked back my way.

"Oh Magna, you will have wonderful, carefree days in our new home. You are going to see and live among some of God's most beautiful miracles on earth."

I looked up at mother in the dark and I asked,

"What is the name of this wonderful new place we will call home Mother?"

Mother's smile came across her face once again but this time the tears in her eyes were large and running down her cheeks.

"Its name is as wonderful as it is. It is called Homeland. You will learn so many things there as you grow into a strong, beautiful Christian. Magna, you will learn patience, love, obedience, courage, oh, there is so much you will learn I don't even know where to start. You will learn to love human kind as you thought you never could. You will love and I mean truly fall in love with some of God's most wonderful creations. The most wonderful thing, my little Magna, is that you will grow in love with our Lord as you thought you never could. Magna, Homeland itself will be engraved in your heart for the rest of your life. There is a sea river we all call Lovestream. It's called that because it's the sea river that streams us home to our loved ones. It takes us home. Along the way it narrows into the settlement valley where you will see each home with its own waterfall. Small farms for each family sit side by side on the grassy hills and the fresh water streams that flow along the side of the river. The temple at the top of the mountain ledge with its ancient columns and its beautiful statues is where you will study and worship and learn all you need to know about becoming a good gladiator for Christ. Oh, Magna!"

As my Mother's story of our wonderful new home and our amazing new future continued, my eyelids became heavier. I placed my head on my crunched up blanket pillow so I could look at the stars as Mother told her story. Yes, the stars were very brilliant tonight but as my eyes got heavier, the stars became dimmer, and I watched them closely as I listened to Mother. There was so much wonderment in Mother's voice, it calmed me. The longer she continued I realized that I no longer noticed the huge wall of waves from the sea or its power as it continued to bound our small vessel. Mother's story almost seemed as if it became a soft song to my ears. I listened to the fairytale songlike story until I drifted into a dreamlike sleep. Yes, I was now dreaming of Homeland.

CHAPTER FOUR

EVAN

The rest of the weekend was very quiet and sombre. Father and I did not speak to each other except to give each other a nod or a hum—and, of course, a couple of "yes sir's" and "no sir's" on my part. There were just looks and glances at each other. Father went about doing odds and ends in the house. I, unlike my father, could not really find anything to keep me busy enough to keep me from thinking about Mother and Magna. I worried about them being on the sea alone. The winds had been up all weekend. I knew Mother could handle the small yacht Father sent them off in but she had always stayed close to the shore lines. I had never known her to go out to the open sea. I guess I thought of every thing that could go horribly wrong. Oh I forgot, God was supposed to be with them, but I didn't understand why God put them out there anyway, so I was dealing with this as well.

As I stood there watching Father, I wondered if he was having the same trouble I was. There was not one step in the house I could make without seeing reminders of my Mother and Magna. All weekend ghostly impressions haunted me. To get away from them I would turn to the double back door that looked out onto the large porch balcony. The porch hung over a rocky cliff with the beach right under it, so there was always a good breeze coming through from the sea.

I was okay as long as I didn't look at Mother's wicker rocker. That's where you could always find her reading her Bible or mending our clothes, or just looking out at the sea with that smile of hers, sipping a hot cup of tea. She loved it out here the best. Mother would always say she felt close to God when she sat out here. I guess that is why I could handle the porch better than any other place. Out here made me feel close to her.

The longer I watched the sea I realized somehow I could handle this emptiness better than I thought. I was beginning to see visions of all kind of imagines of them. I could imagine anything I wanted to, that they were safe, the thoughts of the sea swallowing them up just hurt too badly. No, I couldn't think of that.

The one thing I couldn't handle without trying to make sense of everything was the empty stillness of where they had once been. This haunted me. It was hard for me to handle the thought of living here without Mother. I knew I would always be here waiting for her. Someday she would return. Someone must watch after the house and her things until she gets back. I was sure it would be me.

There was something I had been worrying about. How was I going to look after Snow Cap and Fin Tale? I would catch their food but Magna always fed them. She was the only one who could get close to them. I couldn't ask Father to help me, for he didn't know anything about them. You see, this was Magna's and my secret. Snow Cap was a killer whale. On his top fin he had a strange white covered tip. It looked liked a black mountain with snow at the top of the mountain. Fin Tale was a dolphin with part of one of his tale fin flippers missing. He must have gotten in the way of a shark, or either a marine boat. As I stood there looking out at the open sea I realized that I had not seen them since Mother and Magna had left. I began to wonder if this was an omen of some kind. As I watched the sea get wilder and wilder my heart began to pound again. I would have to take deep breaths of sea air as it blew off the shore just to get the smell of Mother's perfume out of my nose. Her sweet smell smothered me as it filled the house.

I was beginning to feel a little better when out of nowhere the stillness of the quiet house shattered.

"Evan! Evan….Evan!"

It was Father calling me. I started to turn to go to him but he was right there with me. He had his hand on my shoulder, shaking me and calling my name. It startled me. I was not sure if I wanted Father to embrace me in any way at all, so I harshly pulled away from him and walked over to the railing of the porch. Standing there I could get more wind in my face. It seemed to help me breathe better. Every time I got close to Father my heart would start pounding in my chest. I was quickly learning that this newly invading emotion was anger. I have learned about a lot of things this weekend that I thought I would never have to know about but extreme anger is one of the main hooks in my spine right now. I can say I don't like it. I can't seem to think very well with this anger business. Every time I get angry my mind seems to wander into endless impressions of painful memories. I was trying to remember something that Miss Beverley told me one day when I got mad at the locks on the doors of the mission one Sunday morning. I was having a real bad time getting the keys to open the lock and getting mad about it when she came up behind me. What did she say?

"If you read your Psalms more you would know that it is better to 'cease from anger, and forsake wrath: fret not thyself in any wise to do evil.'"

I continued to try to open the lock while she was quoting, but the more I tried and couldn't get it open the madder I was getting. Before I could get too mad she took the keys and with one twist of the wrist the lock popped opened.

"See, you can never get anything of difficulty done as long as you get mad about it. Anger clouds your mind."

And with that I just hung my head and gave her a respectful, "Yes ma'am."

Before everybody moved away Magna and I and all the other kids in the church youth had to memorize five bible verses a week. I have been learning the Word all my life, I just never thought about having to use it to explain my life until now.

I shut my eyes tightly together, taking in deep long breaths, praying, or maybe I should call it wishing that Father would just go away. I wasn't sure if praying would work for me anymore. I had been praying all weekend and not one prayer had been answered yet.

Of course I didn't get my wish either. No more than any of my prayers. Father's voice came out of the shadows. This time there was a difference in his voice. He was not speaking in any tone of voice I was used to hearing come my way. It was strong and to the point. Kind, but the tenderness was gone. This puzzled me for just a few minutes as I studied the face of my Father closely. Indeed, there was a strange, crude look upon his face. It was as if I didn't even know him. Then I realized that he was talking to me like he did to the people he dealt with in the city. This somehow humbled me. I guess I was being too hard on Father for it was very clear that he was changing too. Feeling a little compassion now within my soul, I could tell that the tightness in my chest released just a bit.

You see, Father was an American Home Based Missionary. He also had a small shipping company. With the shipping company he could sometimes provide jobs for some of the homeless. He would find them as they would come into the rescue mission for food and a place to get out of the streets for awhile. Owning the shipping company allowed Father to ship in his own food and supplies for the needs of his missionary affairs.

The mission had a school for the homeless children on the streets. Without this school some of the children would never get any education at all. A lot of government programs have been cut in the past few years. Even the public school system has had so many cutbacks that there are some children who aren't homeless who can't even get a place in any school - private or public. Years ago there were a lot of kids that were being home schooled by computer monitored schooling, until that didn't work out either. People got to where they didn't have jobs or money to stay on the internet system. Finally computers weren't used by the average family anymore. Only the government uses them now. Oh, you might find a few hidden in boxes somewhere but it is against the law now to have one. Father turned his in a few years ago to the authorities.

In the past year the attendance at the mission school has increased. Father asked some of the teachers from the township schools who lost their jobs to help out, but, of course, they would have to help out without pay. This made it hard for them to take on the task. You can't blame them much. They had to help feed and take care of their families or they would become one of the very people they were trying to help. I guess Father was right about one thing. I have seen a lot of changes in people's lives lately.

You would think that they would want to help at least part-time but there was only one that offered, Miss Beverley Nathaniel. Miss Beverley was a great teacher. She was born in Israel. She came to the United States when she was about my age. Her Father is a very successful businessman in the stock market. Her father is so good at it that he pulled almost everything he had right before the economy went down. Mr. Nathaniel pulled just enough to protect him and his family from being ruined. He actually came out better than most.

Mr. Nathaniel said he saw it in the word of God, and, as always, God protected him and his family. That is why he is always donating funds to support Father's Christian causes. He says that it was the least he could do after what God had done for him. I remember him talking to Father one night at the mission as Father was thanking him and writing him out a receipt for one of his large gifts. Father was going through his usual routine of telling Mr. Nathaniel that he did not have to keep doing this every month. This time, however, the conversation was different.

"Well, Brother Straut, do you remember that Bible study book you gave me about two years ago? Well, I have been studying that thing everyday. That book, along with the Word of our Lord has opened my whole world. About a year ago I was studying and I came across this scripture in the Book of James. That scripture bothered me for the longest time. I would go back and forth to that chapter until one day I just knew what to do. Any other time I would have been very foolish to do what I did, but I had no doubt about what God wanted, and Brother Straut, if I had not gotten to the phones and called my broker, well, within two hours my family and I would have been ruined."

I remember Father and I both stopped what we were doing to watch the joy in Mr. Nathaniel's face as he was telling his story. As he was finishing Father just had to know,

"What scripture was it Mr. Nathaniel?"

"You know, the Book of James, like I said. In chapter 4, verses 13-14. I know it by heart. 'Go to now, ye (you) that say, Today or tomorrow we will go into such a city, and get gain. Whereas ye (you) know not what shall be on the morrow. For what is your life? It is even a vapour that appeareth for a little time, and then vanisheth away.'

"If you had not given me that book, my family and I would be one of your unusual boarders right now. So always remember, if you need anything, anything at all, you just let me know."

Father smiled, handed him his receipt, and they walked to the door together and said their goodbyes.

Mother and Miss Beverley became the best of friends. I wonder what she is going to say when she finds out that Mother and Magna are gone.

Miss Beverley keeps much to herself. Oh, I don't mean that she was not nice to everyone, and she sure wasn't shy or anything like that. She just didn't trust everyone like Mother did. She knew how too say no. Mother was always sure there was a way too say yes to everyone. Miss Beverley would always tell Mother that she was too trusting.

"You can't trust everybody Maggie. You're going to run into the wrong kind of character one of these days and you're going to wish you had put that gentle smile back in your pocket."

If I've heard Miss Beverley say that to Mother once I've heard her say it a thousand times. Mother would just smile back at her and put her hand to her cheek and say,

"Miss Beverley you're not as tough as you think you are. You've got a heart of gold. You just don't want anyone to know it."

And with that Miss Beverley would just smile back, put her finger to her lips and blow a soft sweet,

"Shhhhhhh."

As I was ignoring Father, he had to try to get my attention again.

"EVAN! Evan, Son, are you okay? I need to talk to you, Son. I have tried to give you some time to yourself this weekend. This has been a very painful experience for us all, but the weekend is almost up and we need to talk about what we need to do from this point on."

Again, Father was not making any sense. He's talking but I can't understand what he means. Do? Do now? Hasn't he done enough? Haven't we all done enough for God at this point? What does God want us to do for him now?

I could feel my chest beginning to tighten. I was going to have to try and stay calm or I was not going to be able to listen to a word of what Father was about to tell me. The expression on Father's face told me that I needed to listen and listen good!

Leaning against the railing on the porch and gripping it as tight as I could, I squared my shoulders back. I was determined to concentrate on what Father had to say if it killed me. I needed to understand what was happening, no matter what it took! I was looking him in the eye now, and Father could tell he had my attention so he folded his arms and began.

"Before I get to the point of things I want you to know that I know this has been hard for you. I will admit I thought I had done a better job in preparing my family in the facts of the real world. We as a family have been blessed with love. We have been fortunate that we have always had each other. Not only that, God has always taken care of us, as he will continue to do. Our blessed family has never wanted for a thing. We have always had plenty, and even more than plenty. That is why now we must keep Him close to our hearts. For a while, unfortunately, we may not see his bounty upon us everyday as we have in the past. There could be really bad times ahead."

Father was watching my face closely as he was talking to me. As soon as he saw my mouth open he knew what he said had already startled me. So he quickly continued.

"Please Son, just listen! I have watched you all weekend and if I am reading you right you are settling in a little to all this you call madness. Well, I want you to listen to me and try not to say anything until I get finished. To tell you what I need to tell you is as hard for me as the decision to follow my heart with the will of God. It has to be done and you need to know everything. No more surprises. Son, we are not going to be able to live here anymore."

The shock overpowered my face and Father knew it. He had to quickly continue for he knew I would not be able to listen much longer.

"I know, Son, but listen. I had to sell the house and send the money with your mother and sister. The money from the house will take care of them for a long time. I wasn't sure I would be able to find a buyer for the house but when Mr. Nathaniel heard about the sale he came up with an offer I couldn't refuse. He also said that we could stay here as long as we needed to, but I told him no. The reason I declined his generous offer is because we need to go ahead and get started with the business that God needs for us to do. Staying here will only make things more difficult."

I wanted to just pounce on him. How dare he sell Mother's home? Feeling my chest begin to tighten, this time my heart humbled me. I was glad that Mother and Magna had money to help them get by. Wherever they were? I guess there was no good reason to get mad about it now. I did have some questions for him though.

"OK. I guess there is no reason for me to complain about it now, is there Father? I guess you have a lot more surprises up your sleeve? Even though you said no more surprises. I know this is not the time to question you, but do you think you could give me just a little more information about exactly what you've got planned for the rest of my life? At this point, as you always say, it would be nice to know what God is expecting me to do for Him now."

"Evan, you and I can not afford to keep two places going. That is way I have decided that you and I will live at the mission."

"The mission, are you crazy? I mean---while I know we work down there we always get to come home at night. It's crazy to be in the city at night. You know that as well as I do. It gets bad in the city after dark. The people that come out at night are crazy and all messed up on drugs and looking for anything to get into. No! No! This stinks! The police go full force all night. I just don't understand? I don't understand any of this at all."

I had been walking around in circles with my hands in my back pockets, trying to keep my new sprung anger under control but when Father said,

"And that's not all Evan."

It stopped me in my tracks. Slowly I turned and looked at him again. His head was hanging down, looking at his wedding band. I knew he was getting more afraid of my reaction to all of this. Noticing the way he was tenderly turning his wedding band I knew that in his heart he was wishing Mother was here. She would know just how to say what needed to be said. I found the words to speak to get his attention back so he could continue explaining the next transition of my life.

"Well, are you going to finish? Or am I going to have to wait on thunder and lighting to come down from heaven?"

CHAPTER FIVE

MAGNA

The last two days had really been the hardest time for me in my life. The waves had been hard to deal with and the storm clouds had been gathering and getting worse all the time. I don't think Mother has slept since we left Evan and Father. She has been watching the sea, the skies, and the sail with an ever so cautious eye. We have been at open sea all this time.

I awoke again with the movement of the waves and the sun in my eyes. I was pulling myself off the bottom of the boat, which was now wet because of the waves being so high that they were now spilling over into the boat. Stretching as much as I could without completely letting go of the boat, I realized that the bottom of the boat had become very hard and wet. I was also becoming sore and stiff. The sea had been pushing the tiny boat around all weekend. I guess I, too, had my own battle this weekend and I was sure I would have the bruises to prove it.

I tried saying good morning to Mother, but as I did Mother spoke very concerning back at me.

"Magna, not now! I have to keep my eyes sharp this morning. The sea has been rough all night. Just try to be quiet and please stay in the bottom of the boat today, okay?"

Telling me and asking me at the same time made me realize that Mother was at the very top of her stress level, as Father would always say, so I just did as I was told and tried not to cause Mother to worry anymore than she already was.

While Mother fought the sea I just held onto the side of the toss whipped boat for what seemed like hours. After awhile I realized that morning had passed and I was really getting hungry now. I didn't want to bother Mother so I started for the supply box on my own. Holding onto the side of the boat with one hand and wrestling with the supply box with the other was not an easy task, but I finally got the lid off.

When I looked into the box I was shocked. I don't know why I was shocked, but I was. There was no water and very little food left, only a couple of oranges. That's all there was. Looking back at Mother's face, then back at the box a couple of times I could feel the fear creeping up inside of me. I was afraid that we would not have enough food to last us on our journey to Homeland. With all the worrying I was doing over the food and the sea in all its anger I just sat for awhile and waited for things to get better. I also thought praying wouldn't hurt.

I was careful to make sure that I was as quiet as I could be. I knew Mother needed me to be as brave as I could right now so she would not have to worry about what was happening to me. I really didn't know how brave I could be, but I would try.

All I knew to do was to stay in the bottom of the boat as I was asked. I watched Mother fight the sea till I thought she would faint. It seemed as if the sea was angry at her. Almost like Mother and the sea were at war with each other, and it would be the sea or her that would have the victory.

As the sea and waves grew even stronger my fear burst out of my mouth and I broke the silence between Mother and myself.

"Mother did you know that we have no fresh water left?"

Mother glanced at me for just a second and then her eyes went back to the sea. I waited for a few minutes, then I yelled at her again.

"We're almost out of food too. What are we going to do?"

Mother didn't look at me this time. She was watching and working the sea and the sails of the boat with all her might.

After a little bit of time passed by Mother's voice came out over the wind and the waves. She was yelling as hard as she could so I could hear her.

"Magna, you must not be afraid! If it is God's will our journey will soon be over! I know you are hungry, tired, and thirsty, but I want you to stay in the bottom of the boat! Pray, Magna, pray! The sea is not supposed to be this rough this time of the year! I've got to be careful! We are following the shore line now! If I don't watch and be careful we will crash into the rocks of the shore line!"

Mother's voice was strange this time. It had much fear within it and she was quite out of breath. Mother was right. We were closer to the shore line now. I didn't know whether to be happy or frightened. Again, I did as I was told. I staggered to arrange myself in the bottom of the boat and prayed. It seemed as though I prayed for hours. I found myself praying for everything I could think of. I started asking God to hear my words with scripture from the Bible that Father and Mother insisted we learn. They made us learn a lot of scripture. The only thing was where to start? In my mind I was trying to remember. Oh yeah!

"Consider the lilies how they grow, they toil not, they spin not; and yet I say unto you, that Solomon in all his glory was not arrayed like one of these."

The sea was getting rougher and rougher. I was really scared now as each wave was hitting the tiny boat like a thousand sledge hammers. As I continued to turn the scriptures over in my mind I realized I was reciting louder and louder.

"If then God so clothe the grass, which is today in the field, and tomorrow is cast into the oven; how much more will he clothe you oh ye of little faith?"

My faith was a little thin right now. The tiny boat tossed back and forth harder and harder. I continued quoting my scripture.

"And seek not ye what ye shall eat or what ye shall drink, neither be ye doubtful minded. For all these things do the nations of the world seek after; and your Father knoweth that ye have need of these things. But rather seek ye the kingdom of God."

It seemed as though we were going to not only seek the Lord, but meet the Lord if the sea didn't cease its anger. Me and my body were now feeling like flour being sifted through a grinder. I earnestly tried to remember more scripture. I know! Psalms 28:7.

"The Lord is my strength and my shield: my heart trusted in Him and I am helped."

I though that one was a good one. If any one needed help it was Mother and Me.

As I grabbed the side of the boat I tried to remember even more. All of a sudden, out of the wind, I heard Mother's voice.

"Magna, Magna, I found it! I found it! We're here! We're here!

I started to get up and mother yelled back at me to stay in the bottom of the boat."Stay down Magna, it's safer for you there. Hold on, Magna!

After a little more knocking about from one side of the vessel to another, I heard Mother yelling again but this time she was yelling at someone else.

"Hello! Hello! God's greeting to you!"

Her voice sounded so happy. She was even laughing. I wanted to get up but the boat was still tossing me around so hard I couldn't stand up if I tried.

Then I heard another voice, a voice as loud and strong as thunder.

"Praise to our Lord, you made it! Praise the Lord, praise the Lord!"

The voice was closer now.

"Hold on, I'll bring you in! The Little One, is she alright?"

"Yes! Oh yes! I am so glad we found it! I thought the sea was going to do us in!"

I was trying to stay down in the bottom of the boat but I also wanted to see who belonged to that strange voice. I tried several times to get up but the tossing of the boat would just thrash me back down again and again. Just as I thought I would break an arm or a leg, or even break something like my neck, the tiny boat stopped dead in its tracks with a certain crashing thud.

I found myself dazed for a second. I was on all fours wondering if I was truly still alive. Trying to shake off the beating of the sea, suddenly my whole body was picked straight up into the air. Like an airplane taking off I was now flying in the air. Around and around I went. Faster and faster I twirled. I could hear laughter emerging from the air. It wasn't me laughing; I couldn't even get my breath. The whole world was spinning, from the sea to the shore.

Then my body came to a sudden stop. Now I was floating in mid air and dead still. The world around me had not quite stopped and I was trying hard to focus so that the world and I could catch up to each other.

The twirling world around me slowly slowed down. All the while I was trying to adjust my eyes so I could see where the laughter was coming from. Finally after a good shaking of my head a few times I found myself eye to eye with the most awesome man I had ever seen before in my life. His skin was golden brown and his hair shown like the sun. His smile was like glistening pearls. His arms and hands were like small tree trunks. Yes, this was the biggest and tallest man I'd ever seen. He looked like a statue of a Grecian god. He was awesome!

As I hung there in mid air I found it amazingly comforting to look into the eyes of the giant. With a few wondering looks into the giant's face I realized why the feeling of comfort and love came upon me. The giant's eyes belonged to Evan. The shape, the sparkling blue color, all belonged to Evan.

Slowly, he started to put me down. The closer I came to the ground the bigger and taller the beautiful giant became. I felt like I was a helicopter slowly descending from the sky. All the while the giant was holding me up with his enormous hands which felt like feathers wrapped around my waist. My feet softly dipped in to the wet sand as the giant placed me just where he wanted me

Taking a few seconds to get my balance and slowly getting my first full, good look at this wonderful person, I realized that we must be at Homeland. We had to be! Mother said I would see wondrous things in Homeland that I had never seen before. I can firmly say I have never seen anyone like him in my whole life.

With him standing, towering over me like a mountain, I realized that I wasn't breathing. My mouth was open but I wasn't breathing. I had to quickly take in a deep breath to relieve myself or I was going to smother.

Just as air came into my lungs, Mother came running. Praising God all the while with laughter and happiness, she ran right into the wide winged arms of the giant. The giant picked Mother up off the ground and into the air she went. Not quite as high as I was, but high enough to realize that the giant was not only gentle but extremely strong. The most important thing I realized was that Mother trusted this enormous, highly amazing man. I watched them in all their happiness until a sudden rush of joy released with in my soul and I knew that Mother not only knew him and trusted him; she had great love for the gentle giant. This amazing love was running down Mother's cheeks as it overwhelmed her. Tremendous joy overwhelmed them both. They were truly very happy to see one another.

All of a sudden their joy seemed to pour out of them like a fountain which ran over into my soul. I didn't know this man but their joy made me want to jump up and down on the crunchy beach with them.

Oh, how happy I was for Mother. She was smiling again. I liked that. I know she has gone through a terrifying weekend. She was tired but she was happy again and that made me happy too. As I watched the two of them together I was remembering a few words from a song Mother always sang. Within my heart I could hear her voice softly singing,

"Joy comes in the morning."

Well I guess Mother is right again. No matter how bad things seem to get, if we trust in Jesus our Savior joy will always come. If not today there is always tomorrow. As for today the only thing that mattered is that mother was happy for the first time since we left Father and Evan.

After calming down a little and ceasing with the hugs and kisses, Mother, out of breath and still smiling, looked down at me with tears in her eyes and then she said,

"Magna, I want you to meet your grandfather, your Father's father. Grandfather Straut this is Magna, The Little One."

Gosh, the gentle giant was my Grandfather. Now I know why Mother had so much love and happiness flowing from her. As she was introducing us Grandfather Straut put Mother down and began to kneel down on one knee and opened his enormous arms for me to come to him. I ran into his enormous loving arms and gave him a great big hug. Grandfather gently gave me a big hug back. I pulled back so I could now look straight into his face from my level. I put his face in my hands and studied his face ever so closely. With a great big smile I looked up at Mother and then back at Grandfather,

"Yes, you are my Grandfather. I can see Evan in your eyes."

With amazement, Grandfather looked at me and then looked up at mother and then looked back at me.

"Yes, my daughter, The Little One, she has a lot of wisdom to be so young. This is good. Yes, I think she is ready for Homeland. Everything is good and God is well pleased."

CHAPTER SIX

EVAN

Standing there, waiting for Father to continue and trying my best to control my anger, Father looked up at me and began,

"Son you are not going to attend public school any more. You will stay at the mission and be schooled by Miss Beverley. When you're not at school you will be needed in the kitchen at the mission, on the shipping docks, and helping me drive the supply boats. I will need all the help you can give me from now on. As things get worse, and they will, we will have to keep food and living supplies for all who will need them in town. Of course it will get to where even the mission will run low, or even run out. We will just have to do the best we can with what God provides."

"Ok, let's see if I can understand all of this. So far things don't sound so bad. I like Miss Beverley a lot and I've always liked working on the docks and going out to sea in the supply boats as they go from port to port. I'm not real hot on the K-P duties at the mission but it doesn't matter what I like anyway, so the worst thing I have heard you say is that the world as we know it, in the town we live in, is going to heck in a hand basket and we have to be there to protect and save them. YEAH. RIGHT."

I stood there quietly to myself as Father paused for a minute, he continued.

"Evan, please! Stop acting like this. I want you to listen to me, Son. Now I want you to pack only one bag. You will need to pick your clothes carefully. Pack a few for winter and a few for summer. One coat and two pairs of shoes; a few personal items, and please limit them to only two or three things you just don't want to leave behind. I will try to get our living quarters ready as soon as possible but it might take quite sometime. This way we can keep up with our belongings and still have room for others that come in and out of the mission."

As I stood there I became numb. After giving me my instruction Father gave me a quick look of concern, turned quickly, and then stopped. With his back turned toward me he squared back his shoulders, put his arms to his side, and made a fist of both hands. His head slowly moved upward. Then his voice cut the air in the room like a sharp knife.

"Evan you may not want to hear this but I have one last thing to say on this matter. The Lord tells us to be of good courage, and he will strengthen our hearts. Wait, the Lord says. Wait on Him. (Psalm27:14) Maybe now you can try to get a grip on yourself.

"I have no idea how this will end for us as long as we are here in this world. I must force all the courage and strength I can to obey God's will. You are not the only one hurting. You are not the only one who watched his heart and life float away into the hands of God. We all gave up a great deal this weekend to God, but God will expect more from us tomorrow.

"I love you, Son. You must always believe that. The main thing I want you to remember is that no matter how hard things get for you right now, if you believe in anything, anything at all, I want you to know in your heart that Jesus loves you even more than your mother and I ever could. We show our love to you by being obedient to our Savior, Jesus."

As Father's words became silent once again I realized that he was right. I wasn't the only one suffering and hurting. His heart, too, was breaking. All weekend I had only been thinking of myself. Finally, God had let me see just how brave and strong Father's love for Him really was. For Father to bring God's plan for us into a reality must have been one of the hardest things Father had ever had to do. I understand, for the first time since this weekend had started. Instead of anger I felt very much ashamed of myself. I turned quickly toward the railing and grabbed it tightly and looked out at the sea. I began to cry and, yes, pray for God's forgiveness. I prayed as hard as I could for him to help me with the feelings which had engulfed my soul.

After pouring my heart out to God and to myself, I straightened up my shoulders just as I had seen Father do. I wanted to be as strong and brave as he was.

Managing to put my anger on the back burner for awhile, I turned to go back into the house. I wanted to tell Father that whether I understood God's plans for us or not, I loved him and I would obey with all the strength I could gather. He could count on me to be by his side.

As I entered the doorway I stopped to watch Father. He had a small suitcase lying on the coffee table. I could see a few sets of clothes, some shoes, and other things lying in the suitcase. Then I saw father do something strange. He reached up and very gently removed one of the little golden puzzle boxes from the mantle over the fireplace. I watched him closely. When I looked a little harder I realized the other half of the golden box that connected to the half that Father had was gone.

It startled me at first. I wonder what was up. Father and Mother's golden boxes! What was he going to do with the half he had and what had happened to the other half?

You see, Father and Mother had a beautiful two piece golden box that fit together in the middle, like a puzzle. I didn't know what was in it for Magna and I were never allowed to touch the golden boxes. You know, priceless antique or something like that.I watched him wrap the one half of the box in a soft woollen cloth and place it gently into his suitcase. I really wanted to know what had happened to the other half so I called out to Father.

"Father, where is the other half of the family's golden boxes?"

Father, still fixing the box just like he wanted it, started to explain,

"Well, Son, I guess this is just as good a time as any to explain to you how important this little golden box is to us and to the whole world."

"The whole world? I don't understand."

"Of course you don't, Son. Come, sit down and I will try to explain it to you. Evan, your Mother has the other half of the golden box. She will care for it until it is time to give the golden box to Magna. Your Mother will tell Magna just like I am about to tell you about the importance of the boxes when she is old enough. I feel like you have grown up a lot this weekend and I think you are old enough to understand about the importance of the boxes, or if you can't understand, at least you may have the strength to protect the box if something should ever happen to me."

Father walked over to the kitchen counter and poured him another cup of coffee. "Boy, I'm going to miss your Mother's coffee." Rubbing the back of his neck as he always did when he was thinking, he came and sat down on the edge of the coffee table. Father began to finish explaining to me about the purpose of the golden boxes.

"Let me see, I hope I can explain it. Well, here goes. Son, the golden boxes hold the key to the last manuscript of the New Testament, the Holy Word of our Lord and Savior, Jesus Christ. The boxes are divided into two parts. The reason, of course, is for the protection of the Word. Two souls in one accord, in full agreement must come together with their half of the key. Each box holds half the key. The key, after it is put together, tells where you will be able to find the last copy of our Savior's life, death, and resurrection for our sins. It will also open the container where it is kept. This way, it will arise again for all to hear. This is the only way to assure it stays safe.

Someday Magna will come looking for you and the other half of the key. How long that will be, I don't know. She will need for you to be stronger and more courageous than she herself will be. It will take both of you to fulfil this miraculous task, for someday it will become a most evil world. A world where every man, woman, and child will be killed for even speaking the name of our Savior, Jesus. Of course your task will be completed by that time. You and Magna will play a very important part of this Last Generation until the coming of our Savior, Jesus Christ. I pray everyday that God will send you the help of His angels. For I am afraid without heavenly help the task will be most impossible."

"But Father, what are you talking about?"

"Son, just listen. Someday you and Magna will find each other and restore the two halves into one key. This will be the only way that the remainder of the world will have a chance to accept Jesus Christ as their Savior before the rapture or maybe even after. As for you and Magna, I truly don't know how our Lord has it all planned out. We already have a few CDs and a few such electronics hidden away but we can't be sure that you will be able to use them."

I wanted to speak and Father knew it. With a wave of both hands Father continues,

"I know! I know this seems like a lot for just two people but whether it be just the two of you, or whomever, you must be ready to fulfil what God has chosen you for. The task will take all your faith and all you have to give.

"There is a whole generation of lost and the generation of the straying flock of our Lord. Some day there will not be any elders left. You will find that in the past, the generations of our elders were there to back up the wisdom of the Church. Today it is the children. You children will not be children long. You will have to be about starting your ministries toward the Savior's business much earlier in your lives than we ever thought about starting. It will all be left up to the children.

"If I could keep the children of the world from becoming old before their time I would. If only I could turn the clock back to a time when our children were children and were innocent to the horrors of this world. If I could get today's parents to love their children more than themselves and if I could do or say something that would change the hearts of this lost generation, I would. If I could make this lost generation wake up to the fact that they just my very well be our last generation. If I could wake up a whole generation to make a stand for their country and the Holy Word this country was founded on. If, If, If, If, If, that is all I have. I can't change the lives of the future. I can only try to do what I can to help God reach anyone willing to listen, but I can't change it. I can't stop our Savior from His return for His children. The future of the lives of the world lies in the hands of our children and God.

Our children, You, Evan, and Magna, and other children like you. I pray God's grace and strength is upon
all of you who will try. Evan, the children must at least
try or our world is doomed.   Most of the parents in
this world are blind to the times in which they live or
either they don't have the courage to walk the walk of
our Christ. If things are not simple and comfortable
most Christians today don't want any part of it. As you
can see they have enjoyed having one foot in the world
and one foot on the cross. It has been very easy to live
this way. This way no one really has to sacrifice anything or give up anything. It is kind of like having your
world and cake, too."

As father sat there with his head in his hands a chill
came over me.

"Oh, not us kids? How! How will we hold the world
together until Christ returns? How Father, how!"

As Father wiped the tears from his face, with a
crack in his voice, I got my answer.

"Only by the grace of God. If you seek for God's
grace it will be enough. It will have to be. God's grace
will be sufficient. It will have to be, Son."

CHAPTER SEVEN

MAGNA

About that time I heard another voice in the distance behind us. It was a strange voice, with a strange accent.

"Hello, hello!"

The voice was coming from a dark haired Oriental man. He had a lot shorter stature compared to Grandfather. As he got closer I realized that he was a lot younger than Grandfather, too.

"Hello, hello! Praise the Lord, you made it!"

As he came closer his voice softened as he continued to talk,

"We were afraid that the weather was going to get you. There is a huge storm on its way. I thank God you made it before it hit. The rocks along the shore would have surely crushed that little boat of yours."

"Oh, Chan!" Grandfather said with a half roaring grin. "You know that the time is right. God would have made sure they got here safe and sound."

Grandfather started introducing Mother and me to this strange little man, "Dr. Chan Yo, this is my family, my Daughter-in-Law, Maggie, and my granddaughter, Magna."

"Dr. Yo?"

"Yes, Magna. Dr. Yo is our doctor here. He takes care of everyone and everything here. You can't get to Homeland without going through Doc Yo," Grandfather proudly stated.

"You mean to tell me that this is not Homeland!"

"No, Magna, you have a long way to go before you get to Homeland."

"It's my pleasure," Mother said with a smile and a handshake. "Grandfather has written to us about you and your wonderful work. And may I mention the sacrifices you have put in to the hospital for us all."

With a slight bow Dr. Yo spoke, "It is the will of God that I am here." With a finger in the air, Dr. Yo continued, "When God speaks to your heart we must listen. A wise man listens closely to his God. Agree?"

"Agree!" Mother said with a smile and a slight bow of the head.

Before Dr. Yo could go on, another voice came from the edge of the cliffs. As I turned around and looked toward the cliffs, I couldn't believe my eyes. There was what looked like a girl, standing on what seemed to be steps carved right into the side of the cliff. She had long dark hair and dark skin. This girl was bare footed with a flannel shirt and blue jeans unevenly rolled up at the legs. Her hands were on her hips and she was standing firm with a strong look on her face. She yelled, "Well! I see they made it!"

As soon as Dr. Yo heard her voice he turned, saw her standing there, and motioned for us to start over to the steps where the young girl was waiting. On the way over Dr. Yo called out to her.

"They have arrived and they are fine. A little banged up but all and all, they seem fine."

The girl stood proud, squared her shoulders back, and yelled back to him. Her voice was sharp and to the point.

"Where is your faith, Honorable Father? Did you think they wouldn't, with God guiding their sails?"

The closer we came to her I realized that she was beautiful and strong looking. She was a young, beautiful Oriental girl. She was my age or even a little older. Everything about her was beautiful. Her hair, her eyes, her smile, everything about her was just perfect.

"Well, with the storm getting closer I was getting a little nervous for them." Dr. Yo yelled back at her.

"You would!" The young girl stated kindly but sharply. "You act like you don't have enough to worry about. Look at you, my Honorable father. Your pants legs are dripping wet. And you, Grandfather Straut, your shoes are soaked."

Now looking at Mother and me, she pumped her fist upon her hips and with much concern she let us know she would take care of us too.

"And you two look like you've been in the sea instead of in a boat. Come! You must now come and get dry and warm or my Honorable father will be taking care of you for colds or even something worse."

"But Della!" Dr. Yo said with an embarrassing look. "But Della!"

"Don't you Della me, Honorable Father," with a finger pointing at him like a gun and one foot patting up and down. "I told mother I would make sure you took care of yourself. Every day you put more worry on your shoulders which puts more on me and I'm just a little girl!"

Dr. Yo was waving his hands trying to get Della's concerning temper to calm down. This whole time Della was fussing at us. As we approached Della at the steps Dr. Yo straightened his shoulders, put his fist on his hips, and with a voice of authority, he called her name again.

"Della!"

This time she was different. Immediately honor and respect came over her face as she dropped her hands from her hips to her knees and bowed to her father.

"Della, I want you to meet our special newcomers. This is Grandfather Straut's daughter-in-law Maggie and her daughter Magna Straut."

With a humble bow partnered with a sweet smile, "Yes, Honorable Father." Della, speaking softer now, "I am honored to meet you. We have been waiting on your arrival for weeks now. I am glad God set your sail ahead of the storm."

Della and I now were looking eye to eye. I think we were measuring each other up or something. At this point I really didn't know what was going on.

"Now that the introductions are over, can I please urge you all to come and take care of yourselves? If there is one thing we don't tolerate around here it's babying some one when they know better. We all pull our weight around here. It just seems like I'm the only one who remembers this!"

Della's voice was beginning to show authority again and this time her father acknowledged it.

"I must apologize for my daughter's demanding manner but after losing her mother to the Lord last year there have been many responsibilities Della has had to take charge of. She had to take on much more than most children her age. I am proud to say she has done a wonderful job at it too. Her Honorable father is well pleased, but again, I must agree with her at this point. The temperature is dropping and the Little One and Miss Maggie need to get out of those wet clothes."

Then he turned to give Della her instructions.

"Della, you take Magna on ahead. Grandfather, Maggie, and I will get their personal things and secure the boat in the cave at the end of the beach. Now go! Off with the both of you! Go!" With a flip of his arm he demanded, "Off with you now."

Della motioned for me to step up on the step where she was. She extended her hand to give me a hand up. After getting even with Della on the steps she just stared at me. She was also waiting for the others to get a little distance away. You could tell by the sharp look back and forth from the adults to me. With the others well on their way now, Della, with a nice but to the point voice started.

"You look kind of little to me. I guess that's why they call you 'The Little One with Great Wisdom.' You don't look so wise to me."

Living in the city, I had learned that right now I needed to stand my ground with Della. It would be now or never. Finally, the words came to me.

"Do you have to be big to be wise? Besides, Della, I never said I was wise. I'm sure you know more about what's going on than I do. I promise I have no idea why I'm even here. I've only been obeying my parents and doing as I was told. One day I'm at home, happy, and now I'm here, wet and tired. Really, you know more about what's up than I do."

Piercing me with eyes that could stab me to death she said "What's up? What does that mean? What's up!"

I murmured something that sounded like mush coming from a mouth that was full of cotton, "Yeah, you know. What's up! Huh, huh, you know, wise, I'm not wise about anything! I don't know anything about anything."

"Oh, I though you were making fun of me or something!" Finally a smile came forth from Della and her tightness softened. She was in a much nicer mood now. "You don't? You are supposed to be The Chosen One."

"Chosen One, Chosen for what?" My squeaky voice replied.

"Well, if you don't know, I sure don't. You know, you'd better be worth all the sacrifices my Honorable Father has given for you. There is something special you are expected to do for our Savior Jesus. I'm not sure just what, but something big and important. The Council will want to know more about you. Oh, I don't know! We will find out much later. By the way, I'm fourteen years old. How old are you?"

"I'm twelve." I replied with a smile.

"Ha! I knew it. I am your elder. You just do as I say and you will be okay."

Looking up at the steep steps, Della gave a short happy, "Beat you to the top!"

With that, our friendship began. I knew she wanted us to get on our way but I was still wondering what she meant about me being worthy and chosen. And what did any of this mean? And what did any of this have to do with me? Noticing I was already behind, I took off up the steep, rocky staircase after her.

CHAPTER EIGHT

EVAN

Father took a few minutes to take a deep breath and then he continued.

"Another thing Evan, I want you to know that your mother and Magna are going to be just fine. They are on their way to a most wonderful place. So please, Son, don't worry about them any longer. I won't ask you not to miss them being with us, for we will always miss them, but please don't worry about them."

Father continued to explain. He told me how he and Mother had been practicing for months on her sailing skills, and how she would make a great captain of any sea worthy vessel. The journey was only to take a couple of days to get there and they had plenty of food and water. As Father was finishing up, I found myself relieved but anxious to know where Mother and Magna were. I had to interrupt him and ask.

"Where Father? Where are Mother and Magna? Please tell me!"

"Oh Evan, they are on their way to ------."

Father's voice stopped cold. He turned his head to look at the clock on the fireplace mantle. I looked at the clock too, and the hands of the clock were pointing to a quarter after three p.m. Father then turned back and looked at me straight on and smiled. Then he broke the silence once again.

"I wouldn't be a bit surprised if they have already arrived. NO! I wouldn't be surprised at all."

Now sitting on the edge of my chair, I started begging.

"Father where? Where are they? Are they going to be alright?

"Yes, Son! If everything went as planned they are safe and close to home where they truly belong. You see, Evan, for me and your mother, this is not our home. We came here to start our ministry. Your mother and I were born far away from here, in Alaska.

We grew up there together, fell in love, and married. We fortunately were raised in one of the most beautiful places on earth .Your mother and Magna are on their way to Homeland. There they will be safe and out of harm's way while your mother and the Homeland church train Magna for her responsibility to the chosen cause. Yes, thank God they will be safe from all the ugly things here in this part of our world. It is in this world that I must prepare you for your chosen cause for our Christ."

I slowly sat back in the chair, realizing for the first time all weekend that I felt a true peace come over me. Although it only lasted for a few minutes it felt great! It just didn't last long enough.

Father had gotten up to close his suitcase. After securing the latches on the rather small piece of luggage he walked out onto the porch. He went straight to the railing and leaned up against it. He was looking out at the sea in such a way as if he was looking for something. Meanwhile, my mind was shouting at me!

How does Father really know if Mother and Magna are okay? I got up straight away, out of the chair, and rushed to Father's side on the porch. Tapping him on the shoulder I excitedly just asked him.

"How will we know for sure that Mother and Magna made it to this Homeland safely? Will we be getting a phone call or do we have to wait on the mail?"

Father leaned down on the banister with one fist holding his face and turned his eyes back at me. He smiled this funny crooked kind of smile and then I couldn't believe my ears.

"How? Why, Evan, I am surprised at you. I think you and Magna have a couple of friends you've been caring for, for many years now. I think your mother and I have overheard enough that I can get the names right. I am sure that Fin Tale and Snow Cap are with your mother and Magna."

"What!"

"I am sure one of them would have come back by now if something had gone terribly wrong."

"But!"

"Phones? Nope! There are no phones at Homeland. Not even a ham radio station. No, when you're at Homeland you have to truly rely on God to get the message in and out. Besides, with Snow Cap and Fin Tale on the job, and God watching over them, the sea doesn't have a chance."

I stood there with my mouth open and my breath ceased. Having to close one and start the other back up in rhythm with a heavy gulp, I finally murmured a short,

"But how—how long have you ---- known?"

Father interrupted me as he straightened himself up and laughed.

"Why, Evan, your mother and I have always known about Snow Cap and Fin Tale. Of course, Snow Cap to us was Golgotha and Fin Tale was known as Abe, short for Abraham. They came with us when your mother and I first came here to start our ministry. They were your mother's and my pets when we were growing up at Homeland. Why do you think they took up with you and Magna? They have been watching after you and Magna all your lives. I must say, YOU and Magna and God have taken very good care of them, but it is also time for them and their families to go home. Just like Mother and Magna. Just like us all, they too have to fulfil God's plans for their lives. Every creature on earth has its purpose."

Father smiled and brushed his hand on my head. As he turned to go back into the house he had one last thing he needed to know.

"Evan, this weekend has been tough. Are you and I okay?"

Humbly I said, "Sure Father, we're okay."

"Then come, we must get you packed up. We leave for the city and the mission tomorrow morning."

Surprised, I found myself calm within my soul. I realized something for the first time this whole awful weekend. God and my father were watching over us all, the whole time. Even with all the anger I had within me God was still answering my prayers. Mother and Magna were going to be just fine.

Just think, Snow Cap and Fin Tale are with them, safe and sound. Father had explained a lot of things. I still didn't understand everything and I still don't know what the rest of my life's plan is, or what it will end up like. But if I could just hold on to one of Mother's favorite scriptures, I just might make it. Let's see, I think, let me see, yeah I remember. 'For his anger endureth, but a moment, in his favour is life. Weeping may endure for a night, but joy cometh in the morning.' (ps.30:5)

As I watched the sea with my head in my hands and my elbows leaning on the railing, I felt a truly lasting peace for the first time all weekend. What about Father and Mother? They're really something. To think, they knew about Snow Cap and Fin Tale all this time. Boy, Magna and I thought it was our own special secret. Awesome!

Well, morning would be here before you could count to ten. I guessed I'd better go and get packed. I assumed Father would want to leave very early in the morning.

I already knew what personal things I just couldn't leave behind. My baseball and glove, of course, was my first choice. And on my nightstand was a picture of the four of us out on the beach. I wanted to always remember us together as a family. I hope I don't forget what they look like? I hope they won't be gone too long. Surely it won't be too long before they come looking for me and Father? I quickly got the rest of my things together in my large duffel bag. It was time for bed now that I had everything packed. I fell asleep thinking of Mother. I couldn't make up my mind if I was happy that she was alright or whether I was sad because I missed her so terribly. I guess it was a lot of the both.

Just as I suspected, morning came very quickly, quicker than I'd wanted it to. I got up and got dressed slowly, while all around my room I kept seeing ghostly impressions of all my special memories of Mother and Magna.

I saw images of Magna playing a game of chess with me across the bed. We liked seeing who would win the most games on any good rainy day when we couldn't go out. For a girl she was pretty good at it too. She beat me more than a few times.

As I was putting the last of my things in my back pack I almost thought I could see Mother at my desk writing one of her 'How proud of you I am cards,' and leaving it for me to find. She did it all the time. It was just her way. You know, one of those special perks that you never forget.

I tried to shake off my last ghostly images for I knew Father would be waiting for me downstairs and be ready to leave. He said we would need a good night's sleep before getting ready to face our work this morning. Going out the bedroom door, I took one more lasting look of my special place, my bedroom for 14 years. It and I have been through a lot together, but no more. I will have to be strong and surely brave enough to endure the mission as my safe haven. The mission is, of course, the only safe place to be in the city, especially at night. That is, except for the police station and the fire department. The city is a pretty nasty place to be in at night. Anything and all that doesn't come out in the daytime comes out at night. I don't need or even want to think about that right now. I guess I need to get started. If I just keep standing here my newly chosen life will never get started.

Wiping the one tear I was shocked was coming down my face, I shut my bedroom door. I was now ready to give up the past and start on my future. Only God knows how it is going to turn out. God willing I pray I please him and everyone I care about. If it's got to be this way I don't want to let anyone down, especially Mother or Magna. Father said one day Magna would be back but he never said anything about Mother. If I never see her again on this earth I want to make her proud of me until we get to heaven together.

CHAPTER NINE

MAGNA

Of course Della made it to the top of the steps first. She was used to the steep steps. My sea legs just wouldn't allow me to catch up, but it seemed to please Della that she won. I was glad that she was happy for herself. I never was one who had to be first all the time. I think for Della it was important for her to get things right and be on top of everything and everyone's needs.

When I reached the top of the steep, rocky steps I beheld a view of wonderment. I couldn't believe what I was seeing. Out of breath from the run up, bent over with hands on my knees, the awesome sight was just breathtaking.

Slowly I managed to right myself and still my eyes were startled as I was trying to take in the picture of the most wondrous and amazing sights I had ever seen. Walking slowly so I could take every sight in, there were what seemed to be acres of slightly rolling land with the greenest grass all perfectly arranged. Pastures fenced off in just the right places, tall evergreens which seemed to be as tall as skyscrapers. Trees of all kinds, apple, orange, pear, lemon, even coconut trees and grapevines hanging in large, glistening bunches in the sun. Flowers of every kind and of every color you could imagine.

There was a wide pebble road with an arched bridge that stood over a fast moving stream flowing underneath it. As I made my way to the bridge I stood there looking over into the clearest stream water. There were all different kinds of fish happily playing in the flow of the water. This was great!

Della and I walked slowly on toward a large Spanish style house in the distance. I was overwhelmed even more at the presences of all the animals, animals of every kind. There were horses, cows, and sheep. Over to the left were buffalo, deer, giraffes, and even elephants. I really thought I was in shock. I couldn't believe what I was looking at. How could this be? Where did all of them come from? My mind was jumping off the scales.

The plateau we were on didn't seem to be that big, but the way Dr. Yo had everything arranged made plenty of room for everything and every wonderful creature. My heart was overwhelmed. I felt like the Lord was letting me know what it must have been like in the Garden of Eden. With the sight of it all I could say, and I kept saying it over and over, was,

"Awesome! Wow!!!!!!" Della and I didn't speak to one another on our walk towards the big house. Della just watched me and giggled. She had to keep pulling on my arm to assure I didn't faint or something. She also, of course, made sure I stayed on the path and continued in the right direction of the house. I wanted to see, hear, and touch all the beauty that I was surrounded by.

The closer we got to the large Spanish ranch home, I noticed a large sign hanging from the huge oval arched entrance. The wording was simple. In large letters it read "HOMELAND MISSION AND HOSPITAL."

A gasp of breath filled my lungs and as I turned to speak Della's voice, soft and gentle, interrupted me from over my shoulder, into my ear.

"Bet you think this is Homeland? Well, it is wonderful but this is not Homeland."

"I know this is not Homeland," I replied, "but how could anything be more beautiful than this?"

"I know, I too thought the same thing when I first came here. I've been here a little over a year now, but believe me; Homeland is even grander than this. Homeland is like all the beautiful things in the world wrapped up into one place. Of course, honorable Father has only taken me there once. We don't live at Homeland, we live here. He needs me here to help him. He couldn't get along without me, you know. Come now, we have to go through here first. Every man, woman, child, animal, everything must come here to the mission hospital before they can go on to Homeland."

We both just stood there together. Me, standing still in awe of myself, trying to take in as much of the overwhelming sights as I could while also trying to imagine any place being more beautiful than this. As Della stood there with her hands on her hips, grinning from ear to ear at my mouth hanging open, she finally broke the silence.

"Magna, if you think this is beautiful, just wait until after supper. I'll show you something that I think is much more beautiful than all this put together. Come now, we need to get you out of those wet clothes and into something more suitable and dry. By the time we do that everyone else will be here, ready and waiting for a good meal and a good night's rest. We don't only get up early around here; we go to bed early too. Come now! You are going to have to learn to take care of yourself. Around here we don't allow any babying from anyone!"

With a gentle smile at each other we started through one of the huge doors that led into the mission hospital. They both had a huge red ribbon with just a sprig of evergreen wrapped in the knot. They reminded me that this Christmas was gong to be the worst ever without Father and Evan. The door was so large and heavy that Della had to use her shoulder to push it open. Once inside the mission, it was enormous. The pebble path road continued into the entrance of the building. After getting all the way in, the floor turned into shimmering clean, white marble. There was a large rock fireplace that went all across the back wall, except for the two giant windows on each side.

There was a fire gleaming and crackling so intensely that not only did its warmth spill into the mission, the fire lit up the whole room. To the right of the fireplace was a giant Christmas tree. It didn't have a lot of ornaments but it did have all kinds of stars and angels made of paper. I recognized it as Origami, the art of Japanese paper folding. We had learned how to do it in school. There were no presents under the tree. I found that to be sad. I don't know why, I just did. Maybe the tree was the gift? It was beautiful.

Della was giving me instructions as she took off into another part of the mission.

"Magna, you go to the fireplace and warm yourself. We don't want you getting the sniffles, or even something worse. Honorable Father has got enough to do around here besides taking care of you and a cold." Away she went, down a long hallway, which seemed to go on forever.

I walked over to the fire and sat down on a hand carved stool. It was beautiful! It was just the right height to sit in front of the fireplace and get warm. Della was right, the fire was warm and toasty against my wet clothes, and my hair was still damp.

It was but a few short minutes when Della came back with a couple of towels.

"Here! These will help. I'll be back as soon as I get your room up to par. Most of it is ready; I just need to get you some dry clothing more suitable for this part of the country. I'll be back in a flash." And off she went again.

While I sat by the fire trying to dry my clothes and my hair, again I started to look around the huge room. There wasn't a lot of furniture; just what one needed, I supposed, for a mission hospital. To one side, at the entrance, there was a desk with a large book and an ink well with a feathered pin standing inside it. A book that looked like it had names of all kinds. Behind the desk, a few feet away, were a couple of couches and two high back rockers. The couches looked like they were made out of tree trunks, cut and placed together just the right way. The rockers I know were carved by hand, you could surely tell that, for the carvings were of scenes from the Bible. They were awesome!

On the other end of the room was a large table with seating for twenty people. It was one of the grandest tables I had ever seen. Even with these furnishing the room was still huge and still quite empty.

The ceiling was made of glass with tree like beams separating the glass, and the marble columns went from the floor all the way to the ceiling. Over the fireplace was a beautifully carved cross made of wood and stained to shine like a new copper penny. The words 'HE IS LORD' was inscribed on the cross beams of the cross.

There was a hallway that went to the left of the mission. That was where Della disappeared to. Della was gone longer this time than she was when she went for my towels, but she soon returned.

"Drying up any?" Della's voice came out of nowhere and echoed in the huge room.

I, looking around at Della, found her standing there, smiling. She seemed to be taking pleasure in my amazement of all the wonderment I was encircled with. She giggled all the while as I took everything into focus. I was going to like Della very much. I found her to be tricky and a lot of fun to be with.

Della spun around and motioned for me to follow her down the hallway from which she had come. I giggled with pleasure. I began to follow her in a slight trot. Della immediately motioned for me to slow down to a walk. The closer I got to Della she motioned at me again. This time she wanted me to stop. As soon as I was by Della's side she pointed to another vast room with another arched doorway. Looking in the open doorway as Della pointed into the room I realized what she was trying to tell me.

There was a beautiful chapel with the same carved benches to sit on. They were just a lot longer than the one in front of the fireplace. There was a huge cross made of gold hanging on the rock wall at the far end. Candles were lit around the room. It was the only light in the room, except for the sunlight coming from the round, stained glass windows on either side of the rock wall where the cross hung.

A table, close to the floor, with a long kneeling prayer bench was right under the cross. Candle sticks, too many to count, were on the table and in a basket on the floor next to the table. Of course I knew what this was. It was a prayer altar. We had one of these at the mission in the city. Father said every good mission needed a good prayer altar.

As I continued to stand there in the doorway Della explained, "This is the prayer room. Honorable Father says we must always walk slowly and quietly when we pass by here, whether the doors are open or shut. We must show respect to the Lord and the prayers that have been prayed for here and sent to heaven. If the doors are shut you must never go in. If you ever want to send prayers up to heaven just go in and shut the doors behind you. No one will bother you in here if you don't want to be bothered. Of course Honorable Father says that you don't need a prayer room, or a prayer altar for Jesus to hear your prayers. He says any place will do to ask for the Lord's promises, but it is nice to know that we have somewhere special to be with Jesus and to be still and listen sometimes. We have seen a lot of people use this room. They go in sad and come out happy. So I guess if a room can do that, it is deserving of our respect. At least, that is what Honorable Father says."

With a look of understanding and full agreement of the respect for our Lord, as well as the prayers of others, I gave Della a little nod. As I stood there, looking in one last time, I could feel and see the reverence this chapel deserved. You could feel the calmness of the Lord within the whole room. Truly the presence of the Lord was in this place.

I slowly turned and continued to follow Della down the hallway. After passing several doorways on either side of the hall, she finally stopped and leaned against the wall and said,

"Well, this is your room. You will find everything you need. Take your time and I will see you at supper." Off down the hall she went again, leaving me behind on my own.

Into a simple, cozy, little room I went. There was one small bed with one soft, stuffed mattress. The bed was made very neatly with a pretty Indian blanket folded at the end of the bed. Beside the bed stood a nightstand with a small nightlight if needed. On the other side of the room was a dresser with a large mirror over it. On the bed was clothing similar to Della's. A white fur vest with leather carved buttons. A red and black flannel shirt, blue jeans that looked liked they would fit, and fresh, clean undergarments as well. It looked as though Della had thought of everything. The only strange thing in the clothing department was the Indian style boots made of some kind of soft, white leather, lined with white fur. They laced up the front and I was very surprised when they fit me like they had been measured and hand made to fit. I used the brush and twine that was on the dresser to brush and braid my hair. Taking my time to dress took me longer than I had expected. I could now hear voices in the far distance.

Again out of the blue Della's voice shattered the silence. "Are you ready for some food?"

I turned around in a spin and found Della's head poked in from behind the now open doorway. I didn't even hear her open it.

"You should be starving by now," her voice rang out, and as always, she was right. I was starving. I quickly followed her back to the main room of the mission.

There was Mother, Grandfather, and Dr. Yo, all standing around the fire, just talking, and they all looked happy and content. As I came into the room they all got quiet again. I felt pretty weird with every-one standing there looking at me.

Then Dr. Yo broke the silence. "Well, let's all find us a seat and let's eat."

We all sat down at the roomy table, everyone finding their own special place. I found it strange that Grandfather was at the head of the table. Grandfather bowed his head and started to pray.

"Our most gracious Father in Heaven, we come to you humbly, Lord, to thank you for the blessings of this wonderful array of food to strengthen our bodies. We also thank you for making sure that Maggie and Magna made it to us safely. We were truly starting to worry about them, Lord, but we should have known that you would have guided their sails as Della so faithfully reminded us. We leave you now, Lord, in this our humble prayer. Strengthen us in body and soul. Amen!"

After the prayer our meal began with the adults talking all the while. I started in on my supper as fast as I could, I was starving. The ham and sweet potatoes looked, smelled, and tasted like heaven.

Della kept watching me. Finally, I put my fork to the side. Della grabbed her moment. I remembered her telling me that she had something she wanted to show me, but what could be so important? Oh, I remember, she said it was the most beautiful thing she had ever seen, so with out any delay she asked for her time.

"Honorable Father! May Magna and I please be excused from the table? I have something very important to show her."

With a glint in his eye, Dr. Yo seemed to know the secret too.

"Yes, Della, you and Magna may go. We'll take care of the dishes later."

With that Della grabbed my hand and started dragging me into the other end of the mission. We went through the kitchen and out the back of the mission through a large back door onto a large back porch and out to the back yard of the mission.

I don't know why I was surprised by the back of the mission being as magnificent as the front, but I was. I again found myself with my mouth spread open and not breathing as I gazed upon one more wonderful sight of my life. I was beginning to believe that no matter where you went around here you would see nothing but beauty.

The first thing I saw when I came out the door was a gigantic waterfall in the distance. It sparkled as the sun hit it just right, and the angle of the sunlight made a rainbow rise from it like an archway to let the water flow out. Again, there I stood motionless and stiffened, like a newly carved statue. With no surprise, Della had to smack me on the back to bring me back to life and start my breathing back. Taking a great big gulp, I found my voice.

"Oh Della, you are so right! It's the most beautiful sight!"

"What, the waterfall?" Della said with a high squeaky voice. "NO! Not the waterfall! Although, well, it is beautiful. Come, I will show you what I'm talking about. It is down here in the cove waters. Be careful! The cliff steps are steep and a lot more slippery than the steps in the front. Careful now!" Della took my hand and led me down the cliff steps.

"Please be careful and don't fall. If I let anything happen to you Honorable Father would never forgive me. He had a talk with me before you arrived. He told me that I had been chosen to watch after you. You are my responsibility."

I was surprised at what Della was telling me. What could be so important about me that everyone was being so careful with me? I had a lot of questions in my head that I wanted to get answers to. I didn't have time to think about them right now, I was doing all I could to follow Della down the steep, cliff steps. She was right on the money when she said that they were more slippery than the steps at the front of the mission, and it seemed to be father down than the others were up.

We finally came to the bottom of the steps and the damp beach that surrounded the cove. At the farthest end of the cove you could see the entrance to the cove which led to where we were. The waves were bounding the rocky entrance really hard and the winds were getting up, blowing even harder than when we started down the steps. It was getting a lot darker too. Della motioned for me to follow her, so I did.

"Come on, we don't have much daylight left! I thought you would never stop eating!"

We ran down the beach toward the entrance of the cove until we came to an enormous flat stone rock. It was halfway on the shore and halfway in the sea. I was sure by the way it looked that the water at the shore line was deep. Very deep. The sea was bounding against the huge rock and this made me realize that we should be very careful or we could get swept into the sea. Father had taught Evan and me all about the wonders and the dangers of the sea. I could tell that it wouldn't be long and we would have to leave this place and go back up on the cliffs. There we would be a lot safer. Especially with this storm coming in as fast as it was. There wasn't as much beach line on this side of the island. It wouldn't take much for the tide to cover the beach line completely. For some reason the tide seemed to be coming in not out. If it was, everything was turned around and we would be trapped.

Della had already climbed up on the rock platform and was kneeling down with her hand stretched out to help me up. She saw the worried look on my face and again she encouraged me. Della was now shouting her words so I could hear her.

"I know what you are thinking, but you are wrong. The tide is down. Can you see the wet cliff wall behind you?" Taking one last look at the rock and the cliff behind me and the sea beside me, just to make sure everything looked okay, up I went, with Della pulling me up with all her might. Now we were getting wet by the spray of the sea hitting the side of the huge, boulder rock. The roar of the sea was so loud that Della and I could hardly hear one another.

"Okay Della, we're here, what is it?"

"Look over on the other side. Can't you see them?"

The waves were very choppy but I looked across the cove waters trying my best to see what Della wanted me to see.

"Where!" I yelled.

Della grabbed me by my shoulders and pulled me down on my knees and vigorously pointed out to the middle of the cove.

"There they are, can't you see them? They are beautiful! The most beautiful creatures I have ever seen. Oh I've seen them from a distance, but I have never seen them this close before."

Della's eyes must be a lot sharper than mine, I was thinking, until finally I spotted them off to the right, in the middle of the cove waters. I couldn't believe my eyes.

Della was still talking over the sea.

"They're so beautiful! Killer whales and dolphins together! You never see them together. Honorable Father said it is a sign of prophesy, whatever that means."

I kept looking at the creatures. There was something about them that looked strange to me. Then I realized what it was. Oh, I couldn't believe it! I just couldn't believe it! I ran up to the edge of the flat stone and began to clap my hands together. Three claps, then one. Three claps, then one.

"What are you doing Magna?"

"It's Snow Cap and Fin Tale!"

"Who? What are you taking about?"

"Snow Cap and Fin Tale!"

I yelled, trying to talk over the roar of the sea.

"You have seen them before?"

"It's Snow Cap and Fin Tale from home! My brother Evan and I played with them from home! They must have followed Mother and me all the way!"

About that time Della grabbed me and pulled me down back off the edge of the rock as fast as she could. We both fell down on the rocks edge. Della suddenly screamed. Turning quickly around, Snow Cap had burst out of the sea and landed tale wagging on the edge of the rock. I got down on all fours and moved slowly toward him. I finally reached him and put my arms around him as much as I could. I could tell he was as glad to see me, as I was him. There was something in his eyes that showed me his love. I knew within my heart that he would never leave me. No, never!

Della grabbed me again and pulled me back.

"Do you want to get killed? He may be beautiful, but he will eat your head off!"

"Not Snow Cap. He wouldn't hurt a hair on my head!"

About that time I heard Mother's voice calling me out from beneath the roar of the sea.

"Coommmme ooon innnn Maaaggaanna!!!!"

"It's the grown ups calling us in!"

"I hear them! Yes, we must go now! You can explain all this to me later! It is too dangerous for us here, and if anything should happen to you I will be the one to regret it!"

Still trying to shout over the wind and the crashing of the waves we gave each other a quick smile and took each others hand and ran back to the cliff steps. Della had to help me back up the steps the same way she had to help me down. Wet and out of breath we finally reached the top where the grown ups were waiting for us.

Dr. Yo started on us as soon as we reached the top.

"Are you girls alright?" He asked, looking us over, quickly but thoroughly.

"Yes, Honorable Father. We are both fine, just wet."

With that Grandfather Straut suggested we all get in out of the weather. The storm had come up quickly but it was just a nip of a wind now. As we were turning to go into the mission Della stopped Grandfather Straut and, with a strange voice asked,

"Did you see Magna with that beautiful killer whale? It didn't hurt her. It acted as though it knew her. I was so scared but not Magna, she just went right out to the magnificent creature. She wasn't afraid at all. It was the most breathtaking sight I have ever seen in my life Grandfather Straut, just breathtaking!"

Grandfather did not have a chance to answer Della before Dr. Yo came up behind them. Putting his hand on his daughter's shoulder and turning her toward him as he knelt down on one knee in front of her. Now on her own level, he began to explain to her once more.

"Yes, Della, we all saw Magna and the love the creatures of the sea have for her. This is one of her gifts from God. It is only natural for these particular creatures to love Magna. They are very old friends of the family. Magna's Mother raised the creatures from the time they left their parents. Mrs. Straut and her family took them when they left to settle into their ministry on the coast. So to Magna, the sea creatures are like family. Magna knows the way of the city. She knows the way of the sea, but she knows nothing of Homeland

and what lies ahead for her here. There are still many, many things Magna has to learn before she will be ready to do her part to prepare for the coming of our Lord, Jesus Christ. We each have our purpose in life. Each of us has been chosen. Now Della, I want you to listen to me very carefully. You may not understand everything now; someday it will all fall into place. You have been chosen to take care of the Little Chosen One. You will learn to love each other as sisters. You will grow together in this plan of God's. You will grow to love each other so much that you would be willing to die for each other. Your own lives will mean nothing without the will of God in your lives. This is why God has brought you and Magna together. Yes, Della, we saw it all, and it is good with God. But you must never put your or Magna's life in danger. And that goes for you too little Magna. Do you both understand?"

We had scared Dr. Yo. You could see it all over his very concerned face.

"Dr. Yo I am sorry. You are right, we will be more careful."

Della broke in on me and demanded to take the whole responsibility for it all.

"My dear Honorable Father I should have been more concerned with our well being than seeing the beauty of the creatures. I am so sorry my good Father. I am so sorry I worried you. Do you forgive me?"

Dr. Yo had a smile on his face now and was patting his Honorable daughter on her head. "You are forgiven."

At that we all looked at each other with warm smiles and together we made our way into the mission. Trying to remember all Dr. Yo told Della, I suddenly remembered just how tired I was as well. All I wanted to do right now was get dry, go to bed, and dream of all the wonderful things I had seen today.

We all went back in to the mission, talking aimlessly about how fast the weather was changing and how fast the storm had come up, and how fast it calmed itself. After we all got inside Mother put her arms around me, looked down at me with that smile of hers, and gave me my instruction.

"Magna, I want you to go and get yourself dry and put on some clean clothes. I give you twenty minutes to get yourself ready for bed. Now off with you. Go on, I'll be there in a minute to see you down."

With that I took off down the hall, telling everyone goodnight as I went along my way down the hall. I did just as Mother asked. I was sitting on the bed combing my hair when Mother came knocking on my door and stuck her head in.

"Magna? Magna, are you dressed? Can I come in?"

"Yes, Mother, come on in."

Standing for a second and checking me and my room over to see if she approved, Mother finally came over and sat on the side of the bed with me. She began stroking my hair. She took the comb from my hands and began combing my hair.

"My little Magna. You have had a hard few days haven't you?"

"It's not been that bad Mother. I'm all right. I miss Father and Evan, but I know in my heart that we would all be together if there was any other way."

"Yes, indeed we would. Your father and I tried every way we could to keep the family together, but this was the safest and surest way we could come up with to make sure no one could destroy God's plans for our lives. We have a very important responsibility to handle for our Savior, Jesus, but enough of that for now. Into bed with you! Oh! Don't you forget to pray for Father and Evan, they will need all the prayers we can send up for them."

"Mother?"

"Yes Magna."

"Dr. Yo said something tonight that I don't understand."

"What is it you don't understand honey?"

"Dr. Yo said that you have known Snow Cap and Fin Tale all your life. Evan and I didn't think you knew about them. We were afraid you and Father would be upset with us if you knew we had made friends with them. I thought we met them because they were lost or something. I had fallen off the smaller cliffs into the sea below where the waters were very deep and the waves were outdoing me but good! All of a sudden Snow Cap came and gently grabbed me by my shirt and took me around to the less frantic waves. There I was able to swim back to shore. That is why Evan and I kept our wonderful friendship with them a secret. If we had known that you knew of them and loved them as much as we did we could have had wonderful times together with them. Why didn't you let us know?"

"Well it's like this. When it comes to wonderful, wild creatures like your Snow Cap and Fin Tale, you have to know how to handle them. They don't like crowds too much. Besides, if I had been around all the time they would have never given you and Evan a chance to show them that you could be trusted with their care. So, as our Lord says in his Word, sometimes one must decrease so that the other can increase. Does it make more sense to you now?"

"I guess. You wanted Evan and me to become the ones that they would trust, and us only. Is it because someday you and Father might not be there to command them?"

"Well, in a way. You don't really ever command creatures like Snow Cap and Fin Tale. You teach them if they want you to teach them and they learn if they want to learn from you. I think every parent knows when to back off and decrease in their children's lives. I don't think that is anything new. What is new is that the world is moving so fast that children don't stay children as long as they used to, and most children have to make it without their parents. Parents have forgotten that they have children. As the world moves faster and faster there will be more and more lives taken, earlier and earlier. It is just a good idea that parents prepare their children to walk with Christ alone. God's grace must be enough to get you through the hard times. Oh, enough is enough about that. I know I've said a lot, but did any of it make sense?"

"Yeah, I understand. I think?"

Turning me around to face her, she caressed my face in her hands. She gave me a big hug and a kiss on the forehead. Then Mother laid me down and tucked me in for the night. I was glad to be in a soft bed tonight instead of that hard and rocky boat. I have to admit the sheets and the fluffy pillow felt mighty good.

Mother walked slowly to the door, turned, and blew me a kiss. As she shut my door she bestowed me a loving,

"Goodnight, my little Magna."

"Goodnight Mother."

I was sure after I got fixed in the bed that I would go right off to sleep, but sleep didn't seem to come. I just laid there with Father and Evan on my mind. I got up and knelt down beside my bed and I prayed just like Mother told me to. As I got up off my knees, I sat on the side of the bed. Somehow it just didn't seem to be enough. Then I remembered something. The chapel! Yeah! I quietly got up and snuck myself into the hallway. I didn't see anyone so I took my chance and started for the chapel doors. The mission was so quiet and still. It also seemed much bigger in the dark. The closer I got to the doorway of the chapel I could see a very faint light coming from the entrance. I was now beginning to get nervous. I didn't want to be caught up out of bed. I was also told not to disturb any one while they were in prayer. Then I remembered! The door! The door would be closed if someone was in the chapel. I continued on my secret journey.

Looking in every other direction except the inside of the chapel took my full concentration. I was trying to make sure that no one was awakened by my movements. I finally entered the chapel backward and let out the breath that I was holding. Finally, a relief of accomplishment fell over me. Thinking that I had made my journey without a hitch, I turned quickly to go to the altar. All of a sudden with one turn I ran into this huge obstacle. It turned out to be Grandfather. He grabbed me by my arm and leaned down to look me in the face.

"And what do we have here?"

"It's me Grandfather. Magna."

"I can see that, but what are you doing out of bed?"

"Well, I really tried to sleep, Grandfather, I really did. And, well, when I couldn't I thought I would come down here and light a candle for Evan and Father."

"Oh you did, did you?"

"Yes, Grandfather. I thought a prayer to heaven wouldn't hurt, and I promise, as soon as I finish, I will go straight to bed."

"Oh you will, will you?"

"Yes Grandfather. I promise. Cross my heart."

"Well, it just so happens that I just did the same thing. I also thanked God for letting you and your mother make it back to us safely. I am very proud of the fact that you think more of your family than yourself. Yes, your father and mother have done a good job with you. You can always tell a person's fruit. Even if the fruit comes in a little slow or has a few stubborn roots to untangle, God's fruit will always bloom and come in with a big harvest with plenty for all. Come, I will help you send up a prayer to God on behalf of your father and Evan."

"Oh, thank you Grandfather."

Grandfather and I moved slowly to the altar and the basket of candles. Grandfather motioned for me to pick me out a candle. I was to light the candle first, kneel at the altar, and pray my prayer. Then he showed me where to place my candle in one of the candle holders.

"Now it will burn for along time. I know God has heard your prayer, my little one."

"Thank you Grandfather."

"Well, you do know that you do not have to go through all this for your prayers to be heard by the Lord, don't you?"

"Yes Grandfather, I know. But I like the spirit of the chapel and the altar. Besides, Mother says it never hurts to find you a good old fashioned altar to take your burdens to the Lord with."

"Well, she is right, as always. Remember, I will be glad to pray with you anytime, my little one."

Grandfather was now kneeling down in front of me with his hands on my shoulders.

"I am very proud of you Magna, and to think you are so young. If Evan is anything like you I have no doubt that my children have done a fine job with the purpose of their lives."

"What purpose is that Grandfather?"

"Simple! Getting you and your brother ready to do God's will."

"I really don't understand everything that is going on, or even what is expected of me, but I promise to honor my father and mother and God. Oh, and you too, Grandfather.

"I know you will my little one, but I assure you, God is well pleased. Now off to bed with you. Go!"

I started to run down the hall to my room, when I stopped and turned back around and waved a silent good night to Grandfather. He smiled and waved me off again. Sprinting back to my room, I jumped into bed.

As my head lay against the soft pillow my eyes became heavy. I was now ready for a good night's sleep. I still couldn't help thinking of Father and Evan and wondering if they were okay. The night was growing long and I had Grandfather on my mind too. I must be the luckiest girl in the world to have such a wonderful family as I do. Most children in today's world don't even have any family. Yes, I am very lucky to have the family I have. They are all wonderful in their own wonderful ways. .

CHAPTER TEN

EVAN

As I suspected, Father was waiting for me in the kitchen. He was standing next to the table with a cup of coffee in his hand. Looking up at me as I entered the room, I could see tears in his eyes. This was going to be as hard for him as it was for me. Looking over the tip of his coffee cup, Father started his good morning the best way he knew how.

"I can't make coffee like your mother, but I guess it will get me started."

Trying to dry up his tears, his attention came to my needs.

"Can I get you something to eat before we leave for the city, Son? It is going to be a long day. Miss Beverley will be getting the mid day meal started for our guests at the mission as soon as she gets the morning classes started for the children, but that will be a long time to wait for a little something to fill the old stomach."

"No Father, I'm not hungry."

"No, me neither. Not today anyhow."

Silence fell between us. Even the air in the room became still and thick. Looking at each other with no words of reason Father finally cut the stillness, as always.

"Well, just standing here is not going to make leaving any easier for either of us." Squaring his shoulders back he picked up his suitcase in one hand and his sea captain's hat in the other. He looked me square on and said the last words I really didn't want to hear, but someone had to say them.

"It's time, Son. Let's go."

With that, we both made our way through the chill of the front door and on to the truck. As Father and I started to enter our rumbling ride to town, we both took one last look at what used to be home. Father and I were now on our way to our new life.

Father and I didn't say a word to each other on the way into the city. Father drove and I just took in the scenery. Not realizing that my mind was really totally blank, I suddenly felt the truck come to a gripping stop. Looking up I realized we were parked in front of the mission. I couldn't believe it. How did we get here so quick? Father and I both just sat there for a minute. Then Father cut the engine to the truck off.

"Well, sitting here is not going to get any work done. Come along, Son, let's get started."

Yeah, Father was right. We could just sit here and wish we didn't have to be here, but that would not change anything. I could almost hear Mother's voice inside my head talking to me as if she were right here with me.

"Evan! Idle hands make for a wondering mind."

"Wondering what, Mother?"

I remembered asking her that one time.

"Too much wondering why takes up too much time and that means never getting anything done."

As always, Mother was right. Work would keep my mind busy and I would not miss Mother and Magna quite so much. Our time apart would go by a little quicker if I put in long, hard days every day. That way, staying in the mission at night wouldn't be so bad. I will be too tired to care where I lay my head.

Father and I gathered up what little we brought with us and started inside the warehouse mission. Most of the last snow was gone and there was only a little crunch of the ice under our feet as we made our way inside. Winters had been very mild for the last five years and the temperatures were getting hotter and hotter every year. Father thinks it has something to do with global warming. However, the mission was darker than the sun shiny sidewalk outside. Standing still for just a minute, Father and I adjusted our eyes to the dim entry of the huge, cavernous building.

The kitchen was at the back of the mission and the church was to the right. In the front window was a fairly good looking Christmas tree, already decorated for all the Strays to enjoy a little of the Christmas season as they came in and out. Father didn't like anyone to use the word Stray when they talked about the homeless, but that is the word they came up with for themselves. I've heard more than one say, "We just stray around with no place to go of our own."

Miss Beverley was over in one corner of the mission sitting behind a small desk to the left of the bathrooms.

In front of her were rows of folding tables, with folding chairs on each side. They were divided into two halves, separated down the middle with a large cape between the rows of tables. It looked funny, as if the space she had for her class room was divided into two sections, for some good special reason. Knowing Miss Beverley, who could tell? All of a sudden Father began giving me my instructions for the day. As he started he walked over to the reservation counter and I noticed there was a stack of books. Yes, of course, they were waiting for me.

"Here are your books, Evan. Please don't forget to put your name in them. I have paid for them up front so these books belong to you. You only have a couple weeks left before Miss Beverley will break for Christmas, so take care of them. All the kids will be getting back on schedule come the first of the year. These are the last of them so it is your responsibility to take care of them. Go ahead now, and put them in this smaller book bag. It will help you keep up with them.

"You will need to get started with Miss Beverley in your school work. At lunch you will come back to the kitchen and help with serving the food. For a couple of weeks you may have to stay only half days at school. It all depends on how long it takes us to get the walls up for our new in-house stations, and whether I will need you to help with the new schedules at the docks."

I didn't say anything back to Father. I really didn't see why I should complain about spending only half days in school. I wasn't real thrilled about the kitchen KP, but it was better than doing social studies. As far as what he meant by building the walls to our new stations, well your guess was as good as mind about that.

Dad took my duffle bag and told me to go ahead and check in with Miss Beverley. He went his way and I started over to the classroom area where Miss Beverley was sitting. The closer I came to the school area I realized Miss Beverley didn't hear me walking up. The poinsettia on her desk hid me as I decided to make an entrance.

"Boo!"

"EEEEEEEEEEE!"

"Gotcha!"

"Evan! You scared the living life out of me. Come give me a hug!"

As I was giving Miss Beverley a big hug I heard someone give out a giggle. Surprised, I turned to see a girl sitting at the second table on the right. I don't know where she came from, she wasn't there before. I quickly pulled back from Miss Beverley and put my hands in my pockets. Yeah, I was embarrassed to let her know that I liked my teacher. Looking down at the floor I started to give my excuse for my affections.

"The teacher is my mom's best friend. You know, a friend of the family."

Miss Beverley knew I had embarrassed myself so she took over the rest of the introduction.

"Yes, Stacy, this is my best friend's son, Evan. Evan this is Stacy Anderson. She and her father came to live at the mission about a mouth ago. Evan you haven't been around much this month, so you haven't noticed Stacy's father doing odd jobs around here at the mission and at the docks for your father. Stacy has been helping me in the kitchen. She has really been a big help since they got here."

Pulling a thick strand of hair out of her half combed brown hair I noticed the brightest, sea blue eyes staring back at me. Our eyes met and Stacy smiled as she tried to show me how tough she was.

"No sweat, Evan, the one thing my mother taught me before she died was if you've got time for a hug, you'd better take it, you might not get another chance to get one."

Although her appearance was a little on the scrawny side, she seemed very kind and wise. Just as I was about to ask her about her mother, I heard the other kids coming into the school area.

"Find you a seat and get out the math copies I gave you for homework. Everybody! Class! Attention please! Everybody! I want to introduce to you, Evan Straut. He will be a regular from now on, so try to get along with each other. Evan is Brother Straut's boy, so you won't have to prove anything to him on how tough you all are. No fighting! I want you boys to know that I mean every word of what I say."

Miss Beverley was leaning forward on her hands, tightly gripping the desk, and had a very determined look on her face. I don't think I had ever seen Miss Beverley like this before. I didn't think she would know about Mother and Magna either, but I guess she does. I don't know why it should surprise me with Mother and her being so close and everything. I bet Mother told her everything. I bet I could ask her about what was going on around here, but I don't think I'll do it right now. Miss Beverley was standing her ground with the kids right now. I don't think she would like to be interrupted, not with this crowd anyway.

All of a sudden one of the boys, trying to make his point, started.

"What makes him any different than any of the rest of us? We all had to find out what the score was around here. Most of us have had to give up blood. It's the way, Miss Beverley, you know that!"

This guy really wanted to make his point well known to all the other kids.

"Tommy!"

Miss Beverley had all our attention now.

"I know all about your gang business on the streets, but in here you leave it at the door. You know that! Now, don't let me hear another word out of any of you! Now! Lets all bow our heads and thank our Lord for giving us another day and to please let us make it a good one?"

I was surprised but everyone prepared themselves for prayer and so did I. It was strange for me to start my school day with prayer, for I had always gone to public school. Prayer was not allowed there.

Tommy was older than most of the kids in the class. You could tell that just by looking at him. He stood about a foot taller than Miss Beverley and he looked like he could probably use a shave. He wore camouflage pants, black tee shirt with a letter jacket. He also had an earring in his right ear. He looked tough all right. He also wore a black bandana on his head.

Looking at him a little harder, I saw something in his face as he watched Miss Beverley get her message across to the class. There was a glint of a smile on his face. Not a mean smile, but a tender smile. After studying Tommy for just a few minutes I realized that he was glad that our brave teacher had put him in his place. I think Tommy was going to be an interesting guy to get to know. That is, if he would give me the chance before he put me in my place with the gang.

All the kids seem to settle down and the class began. I already knew my new life was not going to be an easy one. I just didn't think the fight for my life would start so quickly. Tommy had that look of concern on his face when he looked me over. I was sure he had already made his mind up about me, and whatever he thought about me at this point, I was sure would be the death of me. Or good enough for at least one broken arm anyway.

As Miss Beverley's voice faded in and out, all I could do was think of Mother and Magna. I was also trying to feel something besides loneliness, but that wasn't working either. The only other thing I could think of was if I was going to have to fight Tommy at break. If I did have to give up blood I knew I wouldn't have to worry about helping in the kitchen or the docks for awhile. Surely Tommy would do a good job of breaking that one arm I was talking about? Well, I will just have to talk my way out of going to the hospital today. All in all the day had truly begun.

As Miss Beverley's voice continued to fade in and out, I got a look at all the kids in the divided class room. The class room was as divided as the character-istics of each student, or each clique of students. The class was large, about 60 kids if I had to guess right. Stacy was on my side of the class. There was also Rico, Eddy, Toby, Joey and Crystal. There were a lot more, but these were the few closest to me.

Rico was Hispanic, dressed really neat and clean. Every thing about him was in perfect order, even his books.

Eddy and Joey seemed to have the same idea about everything. Both were wearing cowboy boots, blue jeans and tee shirts. They both wore heavy flannel shirts as coats. They sat side by side. They were either best friends or closely related. They didn't look related but these days you couldn't tell. A lot of brothers and sisters were close. These days if you weren't close to family you weren't close to anyone. People had gotten so violent that friends were hard to come by and to keep.

All the others on my side of the class seemed to be about the same age, except for Crystal. She looked to be about Magna's age. She was an Afro-American. Her blue jeans and tee shirt with a cross on the front were clean, but just a little big for her, but on her it looked good. Her blue jean jacket came down to her knees, and she was a bit shy too. I could tell by the way she answered roll call. She was also the most polite in the class. She was the only one in the class that said yes ma'am. She made me remember it couldn't hurt to be a little polite too.

Toby was sitting at the back table behind me. She was about my age or maybe a little older. She was wearing a jogging suit with a large hooded sweat shirt that zipped up in the front. She had black tennis shoes on. Her very long, black hair was pulled up in a ponytail. Toby was not beautiful but kind of cute for a girl. She was the fittest looking girl I had seen in awhile. Toby looked liked she was into body building, or getting ready to go into the Army or something. She looked like she could even take on Tommy if she had to.

This one clique that sat on the other side of the class was a different story. They all sat at the same tables. They were joined together with Tommy in the center seat, all looking alike. Rod, Petty, and Matt were smaller framed boys than Tommy, but they were all dressed the same.

Gram was the only girl on the other side in Tommy's clique. She sat on the end of the table. She seemed like she was scared of the rest of her companions. Miss Beverley asked her a question and when she started to answer Matt answered for her. I couldn't see her face so good for the black scarf on her head. They all had black scarves on their heads. You could tell they were all part of the same gang. Good gang, bad gang, I wouldn't know until later.

All the kids here had more street savvy than me. They all came from the streets. Father had been able to help some of the Strays families get back on their feet, but not many. Just staying alive was half the battle. I couldn't blame them for wondering what I was all about. It made me a little sad to think I would have to get as tough as these kids, but if I wanted to make it on the streets, I was going to have to get tough enough and keep God in my heart at the same time. For most adults this task was impossible. God's Word was the best weapon I had, but in these times God's Word wasn't enough to keep you alive. Most of the time it was the luck of the day. Father calls it "God's will."

Miss Beverley broke my concentration by calling Stacy's name.

"Stacy it's time."

"Yes Miss Beverley, I know."

Class had been moving right along, but I really couldn't tell you any thing about what the others had been into as far as the book department.

"Class! Stacy and I are on our way to the kitchen. I want the rest of you to open your Bible on the desk and read II Peter chapter one for today's Bible study. Take out a piece of paper and write down the words you do not know. Then look them up in the dictionary. Write down the definitions and we will discuss them after lunch."

Suddenly remembering what Father had instructed me to do, I stood and called out to Miss Beverley before she and Stacy could hustle away.

"Miss Beverley!"

"Yes, Evan?"

"This morning Father told me I was to help you in the kitchen at lunch."

"Very well then, come along. Stacy and I can't wait on you all day. We must get to the kitchen and get started. There will be a lot of hungry people in here in about an hour."

"Yessss!" I released a breath of happiness.

I blow out with a soft whisper of approval on the timing of the day's schedule and started to get up and hustle to catch up with them when all of a sudden Tommy threw the Bible that was on their table on the floor in my path. I had to hop over the Bible as I and the Bible hit the same mark at the same time. I jumped over it because I didn't want to step on the Word. Well, the Bible on the floor thrown down like that was like, I don't know wrong! It made me kind of mad too. I kept my cool and picked the Bible off the floor and slowly walked over and laid it back on the table where Tommy and his guys were sitting. Tommy just sat there kind of half mad and half who knows what? I just turned and caught up with Miss Beverley and Stacy. I figured that was the best idea I had had so far today.

So, off to the kitchen we three went. The closer we came to the kitchen you could hear sounds coming from the inside. It sounded as if there were already people working. On entering the kitchen, standing at the sink I found two old, dirty looking men. The only clean thing about them I think were their hands and the aprons they were wearing. With their dirty, grey tee shirts tucked tightly under a clean, white apron, one was washing the dishes and the other was drying them and stacking the plates and glasses all in just the right places. Miss Beverley moved quickly around the kitchen getting her apron on and heading for the stoves.

All the while she was introducing me to the people in the kitchen that she thought I didn't know.

"Evan, that is Bruce and Stubs over at the sink. I don't think you have ever met these gentlemen before. They live at Cold Wind Alley. They come and help us out here at lunch for a bite to eat everyday."

I gave them a slight nod to let them know I saw them. Bruce nodded and turned away, like he was very shy. Stubs on the other hand gave me a hardy,

"How do you do Evan?"

"I think you know Mrs. Brown from your old school. Mrs. Brown lost her job in the cafeteria so she comes out and helps us with the cooking now."

"Yes, Evan, I remember you. Good to see you again." Mrs. Brown was wiping her hands on her apron as she turned to speak.

"Stacy, you and Evan take the plates and glasses out where they belong. Then come back and start filling the warming trays with the food that is already done. After all the trays are filled, take them out to the serving bar. Oh, what am I going on like this for? You and Stacy both know what to do. You both have been in this kitchen enough to known what's what around here. Now, off with you, we don't have much time left."

Stacy and I took a quick glimpse at each other and started in on our duties. It took me a good ten minutes of pretending I was interested in my new unselfish duties to get up enough courage to ask Stacy about her mother. I wasn't sure how to start the conversation off, so I started with Miss Beverley.

"Stacy, how do you like Miss Beverley?"

"I think she is great. I think she has her hands full here at the mission but I have found her to be a woman that can get just about anything done. Sometimes she can be a little to the point when she talks, but most of the time she does not have time to stand around and talk to everyone."

"Say, is it just you and your dad here at the mission?"

"Yes." Stacy's smile dropped off her face. "By the way, where is your mother?"

It took me a little bit to try to answer, for my heart swells up just at the mention of Mother, and I had not yet made mention of her comment about her Mother's passing.

However Stacy decided to continue.

"My mother died from this freaky car accident. She was on her way to her daily grocery shopping trip to the downtown market. She never made it there. A drunk driver ran up on the side walk and hit my mother and killed her. She has been in heaven about two years now. Where is your mother? I haven't seen her all weekend. I like your Mother. She is so nice. She's pretty too."

It should have shocked me that Stacy knew Mother, but not really. Mother would have made sure that Stacy was taken care of if she knew anything at all about her and her father. With my head now hanging in sadness I started to softly tell her my story.

"My mother and my sister Magna left this weekend to return to the place my father and mother were born-
-"

"Ho, are they on a family vacation? They'll be back before Christmas, won't they?"

"No, not really, it is kind of a long story. But they won't be back for a long time. It was hard to see them go but Father said it is God's will for it to be this way."

"You mean it is God's will for your mother to leave you and your father?"

"I guess you would have to be a Christian to know what that means."

"I am a Christian." She was now looking down at the floor. "I haven't been a Christian very long. We never went to church before my mother went to heaven. My mom was saved when she was a little girl. She told me all about when she was eight and about when she gave her heart to Christ and all the good times she spent in church. She would read me Bible stories before we would go to bed at night. I always liked the Christmas story about baby Jesus the best. It being Christmas doesn't help any when I think about it too much."

Stacy took a short pause and then started again. "But, that was then and this is now. Noah's Ark was my second best. I miss the stories my mother used to tell. Dad reads me stories from the Bible, but they are a little hard to understand sometimes. He likes reading them to me and I guess I don't have to understand everything about them. Dad likes reading them to me, so that makes it ok. It's our time together, you know what I mean."

"If your mother was a Christian, why didn't your family go to church?"

"My dad would not let her go to church, or take me. She would ask him all the time for us to go and to give God a chance but he didn't believe in God, not then."

Stacy looked deep into the big container of mashed potatoes that we were both caring for now. Sadness soured her face and she continued with her story.

"That is, until my mother died. The funeral was very sad. There weren't but a few people at the funeral and it was not held at church. It was held at my mother's grave site. After everyone left, Dad and I stayed by the grave for a long time. Then something wonderful happened."

"Wonderful! What do you mean wonderful?"

"Yeah! Wonderful! Oh, it was sad at first, watching Dad lying over my mom's grave and hugging the grave like he could hold her or something. Then the most wonderful thing happened! My Dad, he started to cry. He looked up toward Heaven and made a promised to my mother and God. With one hand on her grave and one hand raised to the Lord, he promised that he would bring me up the way the both of them would. He promised God that he would make sure that I remembered her and her God. I knelt down beside my dad and I, too, made the same promise. That day I got saved, right there, right along side of my dad, right beside my mother's grave. You know, Evan, as my dad and I were crying out to God and I was looking toward heaven, well, now you may think I'm crazy, but really, I know, with all my heart I saw my mother waving and smiling as she was holding the hand of an angel leading her to heaven."

"Oh no, I believe you. Really."

"My Dad has been a different man since then. Any other time, if he couldn't find work he would be kind of mean and upset all the time. But not now! He walks around with a smile on his face and a song in his heart all the time. No matter how rough things get he never gets mad anymore. He will just smile and say God has something good in store for us.

"As our journey started for the search of a better place to live, Dad would tell me about God loving us, and that God would take care of us. At first I was the one who found it hard to believe, but as we travelled even longer I found myself having to tell my dad that it was just a matter of time, that God would plant us on good ground soon. And sure enough, since we came here, things have been a lot better for the both of us. Dad says my faith has grown since I've been here, and you know, I think it has."

"Geeee! Well, I don't think it matters how long you have been saved. Just as long as you are now, that is what really matters. Looks like you and your dad have taken care of that, so don't worry about understanding everything about doing everything the right way. I don't think that matters at first. I remember my mother telling me that as I grew older in the ways of the Lord my faith in the ways of the Lord would grow stronger. I believe my mother with all my heart. She would never tell me something that wasn't true."

About that time Miss Beverley burst through the kitchen door with her apron in her hands, rolling them vigorously with all her senses in high gear.

"Evan, are you and Stacy about done? There is more food to get out. The guests are already lining up at the door. Let's get a move on it! Now!"

Quickly, Stacy and I returned to the kitchen and our expected duties. I couldn't believe how busy it was around here in the daytime. I never got here to help Father until after school, and it was always quiet and still in the afternoon. Oh, I had helped out in the evenings sometimes during the holidays and all, but not during the week. Sweeping, mopping, and helping put up supplies as they came in for the mission was all I was used to. Now I know why Father and Mother were always tired. This was a big and never ending job they had.

Lunch went off without any trouble. All who came were fed, warmed, and Miss Beverley read the Christmas Story from the Bible while everyone ate. The mission was full. I'd bet there were about two hundred people who came for lunch. It amazed me as I watched the people who were homeless or didn't have any way to feed their families. I suddenly realized if it wasn't for the mission these people would have no hope at all. Looking over the crowd during the silence of their eating and being as quiet as they could so they could hear the story of the first Christmas from the Bible, I suddenly had a chill run up and down my spine. Miss Beverley did have a way with the reading of the story. It almost sounded like she was singing the story instead of reading it.

It was God reminding me how selfish I had been. I really had no right to complain about the way things

were. As for me and my family God had provided all
our needs and there was nothing we were hungering
for. Well, except I missed Mother and Magna with all
my heart. This Christmas would be one tough day to
get through with Mother and Magna away from us for
the first Christmas in our lives. I knew God was taking care of them now. That is why Father and Mother
decided to do it God's way. We would all be taken care
of. For the second time I was beginning to understand
a few things. Or at least I thought so.

The mission began to clear out a little slower
than usual as the smaller kids stood and gazed at the
Christmas tree in the window of the mission. The mission tree would be the closest thing to a real Christmas
tree this year unless Father could talk the town council
into putting one up in the town square this year. We all
pitched in and lent a hand to do our part to bring everything back to the way it was before lunch. It was now
one o'clock and I was feeling pretty tired. Again, Miss
Beverley's voice sparked our encouragement to continue the day. She came bursting through the kitchen
doors and her voice echoed through the mission.

"Okay! Everybody here? Then back to the books
everyone!"

Looking around as if it were very important for
her to see who had or had not returned and what she
was up against, she continued to gather us all together
and get us back to the books. Of course her attempt
to calculate the number of kids that had returned was
for a good reason, for most of them had not returned.

Everyone who had returned was in their proper seats. Yes, class was ready to begin again.

"I hope you all read the Bible assignment I gave. I am looking forward to the spelling words you all came up with. First I will call out the words which I want you to remember and after you have these words and definitions we will see if there are any new ones from your own list we can add. I will then read the chapter to you as you follow along. If you can't remember what the word means, look back at your paper and apply the definition to the scripture. If you need for me to slow down so you can get words you think you have missed, then just raise your hand and call my name. I will be glad to stop and give you the time you need to get what you need out of the lesson. Now, are there any questions?" Looking attentively, Miss Beverley was satisfied everyone was ready.

"Ok let's get started."

II PETER CHAPTER ONE.

1. obtained - received
2. virtue - moral action—morality / chastity (justice and patience are virtues)
3. knowledge - understanding gained by actual experience.
   Practical skills
   Ex: the knowledge of carpentry.
   The knowledge of God's Word.
   Having a range of information on any certain idea.
   Clear perception of the truth.
   Enlightenment.

4. temperance - moderation in or complete avoidance of the use of intoxicants or anger, even food if harmful.

5. patience - temperance patience
   (soberly + endurance)
   patience godliness
   (enduring – same mind as God ----
   being like Gods nature)

6. Godliness - walking in one accord with the nature and beliefs of God, and His Son, Jesus Christ.

7. brotherly - kindly affection.

8. kindness - good will / be kind to.

9. charity- love for one's fellow men.

Not to judge others.
To give aid to the poor and suffering.
Is the showing of kindness and duty to the needy, and one another.

10. purged- to cleanse.
    to purify.
    to free from sin or guilt.

Our humble teacher looked around the class to assure herself that her timely explanation of the vocabulary was received by all.

"Now, did everyone get the ten words and definitions?"

Looking around, no one said anything, so Miss Beverley continued.

"Well then, does anyone have another word that they found that was not on my list?"

As Miss Beverley looked around for any signs of anyone interested in contributing to the informational word list, she happened to notice Gram. She was very slowing raising her hand.

"Yes, Gram! Do you have a word?"

Gram looked around the room at everyone before she gave up and gave her word.

"I can't say it, but I can spell it for you."

"Ok Gram, continue."

"D-i-l-i-g-e-n-c-e."

"Oh Gram, that is a good word and it means 'with great care.' The word is pronounced diligence. Why,

Gram, I am going to give you an extra A for finding that word. Good job!"

Gram got a big smile on her face as she slid back in her chair. You could tell she was very proud of herself.

Miss Beverley continued with the class, "Does anyone else have anything to add before I read the chapter aloud?"

Watching the faces of the class very closely, she stood up and began to explain her theory. "If you do not understand the scriptures, try replacing the word with the definition so that you can read it to your understanding. Fill in the blanks with the definition so you can understand it better. Try it! It works!"

KING JAMES VERSION OF THE HOLY SCRIPTURES.

(II Peter 1:1-21)

1 - Simon Peter, a servant and an apostle of Jesus Christ, to them that have obtained (received) like precious faith with us through the righteousness of God and our Saviour Jesus Christ:

2 - Grace and peace be multiplied unto you through the knowledge of God, and of Jesus our Lord,

3 - According as his divine power hath given unto us all things that pertain unto life and godliness, through the knowledge of him that hath called us to glory (by his own) and virtue_____:

4 - Whereby are given unto us exceeding great and precious promises: that by these ye might be partakers

of the divine nature, having escaped the corruption that is in the world through lust.

5 - And beside this, giving all diligence _____, add to your faith virtue; and to virtue knowledge;

6 - And to knowledge temperance _____; and to temperance patience; and to patience godliness _____;

7 - And to godliness brotherly _____ kindness _____; and to brotherly kindness charity_____.

8 - For if these things be in you, and abound (to be plentiful), they make you that ye (you) shall neither be barren (idle) nor unfruitful in the knowledge of our Lord Jesus Christ.

9 - But he that lacketh these things is blind, and cannot see afar off, and hath forgotten that he was purged (cleansed) from his old sins.

10 - Wherefore (So then) the rather, brethren, give diligence to make your calling and election sure: for if ye do these things, ye shall never fall (stumble):

11 - For so an entrance shall be ministered (given to) unto you abundantly into the everlasting kingdom of our Lord and Saviour Jesus Christ.

12 - Wherefore I will not be negligent to put you always in remembrance of these things, though ye know them, and be established in the present truth.

13 - Yea, I think it meet (proper), as long as I am in this tabernacle (body), to stir you up by putting you in remembrance;

14 - Knowing that shortly I must <u>put off this my tabernacle</u> (my body shall die), even as our Lord Jesus Christ hath shewed me.

15 - Moreover I will endeavour (take care) that ye may be able after my decease (death) to have these things always in remembrance.

16 - For we have not followed cunningly devised fables, when we made known unto you the power and coming of our Lord Jesus Christ, but were eyewitnesses of his majesty.

17 - For he received from God the Father honour and glory, when there came such a voice to him from the excellent (majestic) glory, This is my beloved Son, in whom I am well pleased.

18 - And this voice which came from heaven we heard, when we were with him in the holy mount.

19 - We have also a more sure word of prophecy; where unto ye do well that ye take heed, as unto a light that shineth in a dark place, until the day dawn, and the day star arise in your hearts:

20 - Knowing this first, that no prophecy of the scripture is of any private interpretation.

21 - For the prophecy came not in old time by the will of man: but holy men of God spake as they were moved by the Holy Ghost."

Miss Beverley gave a bow of her head, slowly closed her Bible, and spoke a soft, "Amen." Amen means you agree with what is being read or spoken as being the truth. Stroking the leathered book very softly and lovingly for a second or two, our proud teacher resumed her attentions to her class.

"Now, are there any questions concerning today's scripture? I hope you all understood what the Holy Spirit of the scriptures was trying to tell us. This is the season of brotherly love toward each other. But to our Lord everyday should be the Christmas season of brotherly love."

Again she left a little room for anyone to jump in with a reply, and with a slight sigh she continued.

"If not, then take heed to your homework assignments. If anyone didn't quite understand any of the assignments we went over today please let me know and stay a few minutes after school. I'll be glad to help any of you in any way I can. Remember we will be having our standardized tests very soon. The mission needs for you all to do your best so we can get you all promoted into your next grade levels. On Tuesday nights I will be available for anyone who needs extra help in any subject. Any takers?" Again, Miss Beverley looked for any kind of interest from her students. Not a one responded to her request. Not even me.

"Very well, let's go over our homework assignments."

Everyone paid close attention to our instructions for the next day's assignments. Then all of a sudden Miss Beverley was dismissing the class. I was gathering up my books when Tommy walked up and reminded me that we had something to settle. As a matter of fact, he kind of surprised me as he came up on me very quietly.

"You're not planning to skip out the back door are you?"

"What? Why of course not. Hey! What do you mean?"

"Well, most people don't like to break blood to prove they belong."

"How would I know if I liked breaking blood or not, I don't even know what you are talking about? As far as belonging here, I live here."

"Well then, let's step out side in the alley and I'll show you. You may live here, but you may not belong here."

"Let's go then!"

There was a big lump in my throat. I had never really gotten into a fight before. I wasn't scared of fighting Tommy but I had never stood up to a whole gang before. I was sure that was the way it was going to come down, and for me, I didn't have a gang to back me up. Oh well, if this is the day I die, then so be it.

I followed the gang out the front door. All the other students in the class followed behind me very slowly. Stacy grabbed my arm just as we hit the front door and gave me a whisper of encouragement.

"Evan! Don't be afraid. Tommy's bark is bigger than his bite. You're going to do just fine."

Somehow her words didn't take the lump out of my throat, or the knot that was now in my stomach. It was kind of her to be concerned whether I was okay or not. I continued to follow Tommy down the sidewalk. I then found myself in the alley to the side of the mission. By the time I got there Tommy and the others were waiting for me. They were all lined up in their proper places. They looked like a flock of geese in flight, with Tommy at the point.

I had my books in my small backpack on my shoulder. When I saw that the gang meant to make a decision of some kind I put my books next to the wall of the mission so they wouldn't get lost or something even worse. Father would be very angry if I misplaced my books or if they intentionally got sheared. The mission funds had to pay for my books and I would be punished if I didn't take care of them. Punishment from Father would be worse than anything this gang could do to me. I didn't want Father to think I couldn't be trusted to take care of myself or to be responsible for what was put in my care. Honoring my parents was one thing that was very important to me. It made me proud of myself to think I was strong enough to stand up for what I believed was right. All of a sudden Toby's voice came out of the silence.

"Watch yourself, Evan!"

Then Rico's voice came streaming in, "Yaw! We've got your back!"

For Rico to be cheering me on it sounded kind of funny. He was so quiet in class, even rather withdrawn. I had to look back at him and give him a smile of thank you. For him to be such a small guy he was mighty brave out here in the alley.

I personally didn't see what the big deal was. Yeah, I was scared, but come on, what could they really do to me right here in the daylight, with everyone watching? Looking around and looking into all the nasty stares of all the guys, I decided I had better get myself ready for something I wasn't truly expecting. I think this was going to be a little more complicated than I thought. Maybe I was mistaken? Maybe they could and would do whatever they wanted to. Kids were killing kids in this world. This world was not like my world. But I don't live in my world anymore. I live here in their world. I think my world has died.

All of this was going on as I was preparing myself in front of the flock.

"Okay Tommy, here I am, now what?"

Tommy held out his hand and snapped his finger. Matt stepped out of his place in the arrowed line up and stepped up to Tommy's side. I watched Matt closely to see what his part in this was going to be. Matt reached into his jeans pocket and pulled out what looked like a knife. I wasn't sure because it was hidden in the palm of his hand. He handed his surprise to Tommy as if it were expected of him to obey Tommy's every instruction. I walked a little closer so I could get a better look at what Tommy had hidden in his hand. Matt turned and took his place back in the line up. That good look I was waiting for came as Tommy opened the blade on what was my first guess, a knife. It seemed to be all blade as it sparkled in the sunlight.

"Hey! I don't go in for knives Tommy."

"What's the matter, Preacher Boy? Scared of a little knife?"

"It's not the knife I'm scared of, but the reason behind it."

Looking at me as if he wasn't sure of what to do with me next, Tommy began to ask me questions about myself.

"How old are you, Preacher Boy?"

"I'm fourteen and a half years old, and by the way, my name isn't Preacher Boy! It's Evan! "

"Okay, okay! Don't get upset!"

"Well, let's keep everything nice and clean. If at all possible none of us will have to get upset. Besides, it doesn't upset me that you call me Preacher Boy, for that is what I am. Just seems to me you are trying to bring my father in on this. My father has done nothing but shown you kindness."

"Evan, we are known as the Black Hoods. We're not one of the worse gangs in town but we do take care of each other." Pausing a second, he started back his introduction, "Sometimes that means doing things we don't like to do."

"Looks to me like everyone in the Black Hood has to do as you say?"

"Well, I earn the right to be the leader. I'm the oldest."

"By the way Tommy, just how old are you? Taking care of all the Hoods must be a hard job?"

"I'm sixteen years old. Matt's thirteen. He'll take over if something were to happen to me. If you must know, yeah it's a hard job, but somebody's got to do it. I have my mother and an eight month old baby brother to take care of too. My dad split, leaving me with his job. It's no secret; we all have family on the streets with nowhere to go. We have to protect them from the other strays. If you want our protection you'll have to break blood with us."

"How about explaining to me what this breaking of blood is before you assume that I want a part of it?"

With a hearty laugh Tommy looked around at the other Hoods.

"Oh, you will want to be a part of it. If you don't, you will be all alone on the streets. There are other stray gangs out here besides us, but they'll leave you dead in the streets. Or starve you into an early grave. The streets around here are pretty bad at night. Oh, I think if you think about it real hard you'll find it better for you if you join up with us."

I did take a few seconds to think about what he was saying. After all, they were the homeless. They did know what was going on in the streets better than I did. Looking Tommy eye to eye and trying to buy some time I asked, "What is breaking blood? You still haven't told me."

Tommy walked forward from his position at the head of the line. Now he was standing pretty close to me. It was now definitely personal between us.

"It isn't anything dangerous or anything like that if that's what you are afraid of. It is like, well you know, becoming blood brothers. I cut a small cut in the shape of an arrow in the palm of your hand, and then I will do the same in mine. We put them together and pledge ourselves to each other. So what do you say? Let's do this and get it over with. I've got to round up some work before I head back to the Caverns. I've got my family to feed before dark."

"What do I have to pledge, Tommy, and to whom?"

"First, you come into our clique as a brother. Making sure that all your brothers are safe from the other strays and that your brother has a place to crash at night and that your brother eats before you do. Last, but the most important, is that you have to do what ever I tell you to do. Obeying the leader is a must. Everyone will not get taken care of if all of this cannot come down on a daily basis. Because no matter what we have to do, we do it so that everyone is taken care of."

Thinking about it, taking my few moments to study what Tommy was saying, I had made my decision. Separating my feet and squaring back my shoulders, I knew what my answer was going to be. I had to be careful how I handle it though. Things could get all turned around and someone could get hurt. Like me! Or even one of the other guys. I didn't want anyone to get hurt. So I started asking God to help me out of this one.

"Hey #1, are you watching? I can't walk Tommy's walk. You are going to have to fix this one." My soul started to talk to me. I had my answer.

"Tommy I feel kind of proud, man, that you would want me to be a part of the Black Hood but I'm sorry, I can't. I have no problem doing most of the things you ask in the pledge. That is what my father and I do on a daily basis, but I have trouble with just a couple of things that I think we need to talk about before this can go on."

All of a sudden there were ooooooooohhhhhhh-hhh's and aaaaaaaaaahhhhhhhhhh's coming from all directions. Then Eddy's voice came from the crowd behind me.

"Is he crazy or something!? No one has ever turned the Black Hoods down. Hey Tommy, ask me to join the Black Hoods. I'll take the pledge for your protection."

"Will you now!" said Toby, "Oh be quiet Eddy they don't want you in their clique. Protecting you is a full time job. No one knows that better than me!" Stepping a little closer to what was going on, Toby continued, "This just gets better the longer it goes on."

You could tell by Toby's voice that she was enjoying my boldness toward Tommy. I didn't consider it bold. I just didn't want to have to do everything Tommy told me to do. Then there was this other thing. What if he asked me to do something that was wrong? If I make promises, I will have to keep them. I will not dishonor my parents if I can do anything to stop it. That was what I was trying to do now, lumpy throat, shaking knees, and all. I guess I could blame it on the cold weather. The plain truth was I was just down right scared.

Tommy wasn't very pleased with my answer. As a matter a fact, he looked kind of mad. Especially, with the others becoming my cheering section.

"What seems to be the problem?"

"Well, Tommy, I don't mean anything bad towards you and the Hoods, but I am the kind of guy that likes to do things my way. You and I might not agree sometime about something, and well, then there will go our friendship. Don't you think our friendship is more important than having one more member in the Hood to take care of? Seems to me you've got enough Hoods to take care of. One more would only make it rougher on all of you. Then there's this thing about breaking blood. That could be alittle dangerous don't you think? I don't mix my blood with anybody's blood but my family. You can get AIDS, or even something worse that way. So see Tommy, I couldn't take the whole pledge, so why take it at all?"

Tommy was mad, and I tried not to dishonor him in front of the other Hoods. I think that's the only thing in my favor that might save me at this point. Tommy paced back and forth for a few rounds, and then stopped right in front of me. Letting out a few huffs of wind and assuming that I was going down any second now, I prepared myself by digging my heels into the gravelled alleyway. I was trying to watch every move Tommy was making. Father had always told me to never take my eyes off my enemy. I was trying to remember everything Father had every taught me about standing up for myself. I guess I was about to find out if it would work.

By now, I myself was getting pretty nervous about what Tommy was going to do to me. I started to pray for God to help me get myself out of this alleyway. Then I got an idea of my own. Well, # 1 might have had something to do with it.

"Look Tommy, I really don't want any hard feelings between us, but I am already a member of my own clique."

With that Tommy stopped dead in his tracks.

"You've got your own clique? What clique are you a member of? I know all the gangs around here and I've never seen you out at any of the gang sites before. What's the name of this clique you are a member of?"

Well, Tommy had now caught me off guard. Trying my best to come up with a name I suddenly remembered something my mother was always making me promise.

"Evan! You watch yourself and promise to always walk in the Word out there."

With that I burst out with the name of my clique.

"We're called The Word Walkers."

"The Word Walkers? I've never heard of any clique called that. Come on, admit it, you're not a member of any clique. Your father would have your skin if you were to join a gang of any kind. Isn't that right guys?"

"Yeah, that's right. He's just telling you that so you won't put him in his place, Tommy. Don't listen to him, let him have it good!"

"Just because you don't believe there is one, doesn't mean there isn't. Let me ask you something, Tommy. Are you a Christian?"

"I believe there is a God, if that's what you mean."

"No Tommy, that's not what I mean. Do you know God? Do you believe in God?

"It's kind of hard to get to know God when he is never around."

I was feeling pretty bad for Tommy now. It was hard to stay mad at anybody, especially kids, trying to make it on the streets. Besides, I just came through my own doubts about whether God was taking care of things or not.

"You know, Tommy. We're not as different from each other as you think. I can't always see God either but there is one difference between us. I don't have to see God to know he is around. Just lately I got pretty mad at God, then I realized that it was me with the problem, not God. I have had to grow up a lot lately. Before today I would have been afraid to stand up to you and tell you these things. Before today I was about ready to decide to become an unhappy Christian and about ready to become one of the happy run away Christians who turn their backs on their God and their family. Just yesterday I thought I would be happier running from God than running with God. I've had to grow up a lot over the past few days. Believe me, growing up is not the easiest thing in this world to do. It hurts! You know that better than anyone, Tommy. Just look at you taking care of so many people. You, too, have a great many responsibilities but I'm sorry Tommy, I can't join up with you like this. I promised my mother that I would give God a chance to prove His way for me. I know all this sounds corny to all of you, but right now I don't care. Proving my love for my mother and what she wants for my life is more important to me than being afraid of you. So, do what you've got to do and let's get it over with. Besides, you've got the Hoods to take care of before nightfall, right? And I've got to get back to the mission to help my father. Tommy, I can help you better doing this my way than yours. The mission is always going to be here for you and your family and all the others you take care of. To that, I will give my promise to you and all the other Strays. As long as my Father and I can, we will keep the mission open for all the Strays, for as long as we can. What do you say, Tommy, truce?"

I held out my hand for Tommy to take in friendship. At first I didn't think he was going to take it, then all of a sudden Tommy gave out a big laugh and came walking over to me.

"Why not, you make a lot of sense. For now we have a truce, my new found friend. You've got yourself a deal."

Taking a long look at me with a look I wasn't sure of, Tommy held out his hand and we shook on it, giving each our word.

"You can stand on it, Preacher Boy. Me and the Hoods, will leave you and your father alone, and the other Word Walkers, if there are any more of you. You promise? You will keep the mission open, right?"

"Sounds like I made my first deal on the streets, Tommy, and it seems like it's not such a bad deal at all. It's one I can live with. I promise as long as my Father and I can, the mission will be here, truce!"

"Just remember what happens if you break it. With no mission you and your Dad become strays, just like everybody else. It will be every stray for himself!"

"Yeah, I realize that. Don't worry, when the mission can no longer keep the deal I'll be on my own, and I'm not going to let anyone get in my way either!"

"That's fair enough!" Tommy was firm this time. The smile was gone from his face.

About that time I heard Father call for me. All the others heard him too. Tommy and the Hoods turned and ran out the back of the alley. Toby and the others just weren't there any more. The only one left standing with me was Stacy.

"Well, Evan, you did great. There is only one thing now left to do. You have a lot to live up to. You know that don't you? This will be all over town by tomorrow. You've made your stand with the Black Hoods today, but the others will hear about what happened here to-day and you will have to make your stand with all of them sooner or later. Tommy and his guys are angels compared to the rest of the town. I hope you are up to all this?"

"Yeah, I know. And this town isn't that big either. It won't take long for the word to get around. Well, I can't worry about that right now. At least I'm not dead or beat to a bloody mess. Who knows, Stacy, I just might make it till Christmas after all. I've got to go. Father is calling me. Are you coming?"

"Yeah, I live at the mission too, you know. My fa-ther will be looking for me before too long. Besides, I guess I just became a Word Walker."

"Oh yeah! I guess you did if you're going to walk the walk around town with me."

"Yeah! It would be my pleasure. These belong to you, dear leader." Stacy was bowing from her waist like I was royalty or something, handing me my back-pack that held my books.

All of a sudden Father came around the corner of the mission.

"Well, here you are. I've been looking for you, Son. Are you okay?"

"Sure, Father, I'm fine. Stacy and I were just getting some air and saying good-bye to the other guys."

"Oh yes, how was your first day at school? I hope Miss Beverley wasn't too hard on you. I sure hope she didn't give you much homework. You and I have to get the walls to our stations up tonight. I've got great news! Mr. Anderson and I found some prime wood in a wood pile at the old mill they are tearing down outside of town. I don't know if we'll have time for both deeds to get done by bed time. Lights out at the mission is at 10:00 p.m., you know. City laws have to be obeyed, but how would you like your own, let's see what is it you kids call it, your own place to crib down to sleep at night?"

"Yeah, really Father? That's great!"

Father was right, we needed to get to work on our stations if that meant that we would have our own, private sleeping area, and I did have some homework to get finished.

"Well, then, I guess we'd better get started. Looks like you and I have got a busy night ahead of us. There is only one thing I want to know, Father."

"What's that, Son?"

"What time do we eat?"

Father, Stacy, and I all started to laugh and make our way back to the mission. Father put his arm around my shoulder so he could walk with me, side by side.

"Well, you did have a good day today. I'm glad, Son. I have been worried all day whether you would like it here or not. I mean, I know it's not home, but it's not soooo bad is it?" Father was now wrestling with me a little. He was always doing that.

"Yeah, I guess you're right. It's not home but we're together and that is what counts. Mother would want me to try as hard as I could to give it a chance."

"Yes she would, Son. You have made me proud today. You are truly growing up to have a proud walk about you, Son."

Stacy and I just looked at one another in amazement.

"You know, Father, I am proud to know it is you who walks by my side."

Stacy and I just started laughing; it was rather hard to believe that Father just happened to use that wording.

"What's the matter, did I say something funny?"

Continuing to laugh, I gave Father a simple answer to assure him that his mind was not beginning to twist around on him.

"No Father, as a matter of fact you said just the right thing. I guess that makes us a couple of Word Walkers."

"Word Walkers, hey I like that, Son. That reminds me of your mother. She was always telling us to walk with the Lord every time we'd leave the house. Yeah! I really like that. Come along, Stacy, I guess were just a bunch of Word Walkers! Let's get busy walking."

With that we all started to walk back into the mission to finish our daily duties. Then Father remembered the very thing he needed me for. Coming to a sudden stop and tapping himself on the head, Father gave the word.

"Evan, I almost forgot what I called you for. I need for you to help me unload the truck with the lumber for our stations! You meet me at the back entrance and I will pull the truck behind the mission at the loading dock and you can help me get the lumber inside before dark. Go now! It won't take me long to meet you out back."

Stacy went on her way toward the kitchen and I went to the loading docks. After unloading all the materials that we would need and placing them at the far end of the mission so everything would be where we could get to it easily, Father and I started putting up the walled units for our private spaces.

After the walls were up and painted on the inside we started on the outside. Then we stopped for some supper. Stacy had brought us a plate of leftovers and each a good, cold glass of milk. There was apple pie for the both of us as well. I was hungry and ate every bit of my supper. My plate was so clean I was sure it didn't even need to be washed. I guess that was just wishful thinking.

Stacy's dad had gathered up a couple of cots for us to sleep on. They fit the small space in the room just right. Then Father took two folding tables and put them by our beds as night stands. He put one small lamp on each of the tables so we could read at night. He wanted me to be able to read my Bible, and to be able to work on homework.

"Well, Evan, looks like we did a fine job. At least we can sleep and change clothes without any one to brother us. These curtains will make fine doors for the rooms until we can get a couple of real ones.

The most important thing is for you to remember to always keep your belongings under your bed and locked while you are not around. A lot of different kinds of people come through here every day. You can't trust anyone you don't know. Are you listening, Son? I mean it! You have to be careful."

"Yes, Father, I will do whatever you say. I promise!"

I could tell Father was concerned for me and my personal things. He was right. Although strays, the homeless, were very unfortunate people, most of them were fine people. Most of them had been on the streets so long that stealing was the easiest way for them to get money for their families. Of course I didn't say it was the most honest, just the most profitable. Father was right; he and I lived in the real world now. Not the wonderful world Mother made for us at home. I mean the real, hard, cruel world. One I knew I wasn't going to get along in without making some changes within myself. These changes would have to take place or I would not make it on the streets, or get along with the strays, not for very long.

I took the lock Father gave me and tried it a few times to see if I could lock it and unlock it without any trouble. I put it on my bag and put my bag under my bed and locked it around the iron legs of the cot. I guess this would be my routine from now on.

Father was now directing me to the back door with the trash cans that we filled with small pieces of lumber and trash when we put up our rooms.

"Son, I'll get our beds made and you can get this trash to the dumpsters outside, in the back alley. We need to get the trash all together anyway for the trash pick up in the morning."

Mr. Anderson offered to help me but Father told him I could get them by myself. He wanted Mr. Anderson to get the rest of the people down for the night that was going to stay at the mission. Sometimes some of the night time boarders were impaired on drugs or alcohol and it took awhile to get them quiet. Not everyone stayed at the mission at night. A lot of the families found spaces on the streets and made sort of a home for their families to stay together. A lot of the strays stayed down at the beach in the caverns. That wasn't always the best place. Sometimes the sea would get up during storms and the tide would wash into the caverns. A few people had even drowned from the flash flooding of the high tides. A lot of the senior citizens made Cold Wind Alley their home. The reason they called it Cold Wind Alley, is because it was one of the main, long alleys that ran behind the Town Hall, Police Station, and some of the other township buildings that were always being patrolled by the police. They felt safe in the alleyway, but it always caught the cold sea breezes off the shore lines. This time of winter it really gets rough for them. Father has found quite a few elders passed away from exposure to the cold. I've heard Father and

Mother talk about it when Father would come home late.

Some would even set up odds and ends so they could cook their own meals at these street homes instead of coming to the mission for food. Only when they could not get the food themselves would they come to the mission for shelter and food.

There was one thing that they all did. On Sunday morning the mission would be full for the Sunday morning service. It seemed as though no matter what they had to do through the week to survive, on Sunday they would at least give God a few minutes. Good or bad, it didn't matter. Even all the gangs would come without causing any trouble. The mission was sort of a safety zone with a peace truce attached.

"It's always strange to watch these poor souls come together in this quiet, peaceful way," mother would always say. "All things are possible with God our Savior, even a truce on Sunday morning."

I told Mr. Anderson thank you, but that I could get them, and I started to drag them to the two big back doors that went out to the docks and then on into the alley. The alley was dark. As a matter a fact, it was a really creepy dark. I stood there looking around and that lump was back in my throat again. Standing still, I cautiously watched every movement. I also listened to every sound, wondering. Wondering if I was going to get attacked in the dark or if I could just go over to the dumpsters and then run back before anything could happen to me.

"Yeah, ya think!"

While standing here thinking about it I realized that this was not getting the trash emptied. So into the dark alley I went, dragging the heavy trash cans behind me. At first it seemed like it would take me forever to get the big and bulky trash cans to the other side of the alley. Then, all of a sudden, the cans became light as feathers and I was racing to the other side of the alley with the speed of an eagle in flight, or so it seemed. As I reached the dumpsters I came to a sudden stop, slamming into the wooden fence that divided the alley from the other township. Trying to put aside the fact that I didn't know how I got up the speed to handle my task, I personally put it off on fear. I closed my eyes and thanked God out loud,

"Oh thank you, Lord, for giving me the extra strength I needed to get here safely!"

"Why, you are most welcome!"

"W—H—A—T!"

I was shocked right off my feet and I jumped at least three feet in the air as I heard a strange voice come from out of the air behind me. Jumping and turning at the same time to see who or what it was, I couldn't believe my eyes.

There was a tiny little man floating in the air with both ends of the trash can in either hand, holding them up like they were made of cloth. He was scruffy and had a dusty white robe on. His hair was brown and he wore it in a ponytail that went very long down his back.

While I was catching my breath I sat down on the ground, against the dumpsters. Before I fell down with fright and disbelief I found myself burst out the very questions that needed to be answered to keep my sanity in tact.

"Whooo are yoouuu? Or whaaaat are youuuuuu?"

"Hello, Evan. It is nice to finally get to meet you in person."

"Finally…meet me?"

"Yes! I have known you all your life. Ever since the day you were born. Oh yes, I have. I truly have."

"But who are you? I mean, what are you?"

"Oh! Let me introduce myself to you."

Gently he put the trash cans down and landed softly on his feet on the gravelled alleyway. Now I was looking him eye to eye. He looked as though he was only about four feet tall.

"I am Jeffrey, your guardian angel. I was assigned to you at birth. I have been watching after you all your life. And I have been doing a good job of it too, if I say so myself. You should be very honored to have me as your guardian angel. I have taken care of a lot of people. You are the two hundred and twenty seventh child put into my care. I am very experienced at taking care of God's children."

"I don't understand? Why are you here with me? I have heard of guardian angels but I really never believed they were for real."

"Oh yes, we are very real, very real indeed. We have been bringing messages and protecting our Lord's people since the beginning of time. Oh yes, we are very, very real and we are one of the most important companions in your life."

"Hey, wait a minute! How come I can see you? I'm not supposed to see you, am I? I remember that my mother told me one time that I had a guardian angel who kept me from falling off the back porch one summer when I was about six. I told Mother that I didn't see any angel. She told me that we can't see our angels. We're just supposed to listen and watch for the careful signs that our angels will show us to keep us safe."

"Your mother is a very beautiful and wise woman, but angels have been bringing messages to humans since the beginning of time. My own brother brought Joseph's message to him when he was worried about taking Mary, our Lord's mother as his wife. You see, being God's messenger is a very important task, and a great honor.

"And of course you are right. I did keep you from falling off the porch when you were six. I just gave you a little nudge back the other way to keep you from falling backward. That was a close one, yes it was, yes it was!"

"Why are you so dirty?"

"Oh, I forgot to clean myself up after my last adventure. The Lord called on me very quickly to report to Him. My orders were to get to you as quickly as I could and produce myself to you. The Lord wants you to know that He is with you, and that I will help you whenever I can to protect and keep you safe. Here, let me clean myself up a little."

With that he lifted up in the air and twirled around in a circle and then back down again. Lo and behold he actually sparkled, and even glowed.

"There now, is that better?"

"Yes, much better. That is, if you're real!"

"Oh, I am real, very real!"

"Well, I sure hope so!"

"My first lesson to you is to let you know that I am always with you. Our Lord Jesus wants you taken care of so you can fulfil your chosen duties. You will not be able to see me all the time. I am not here to make things easier for you. In all things in life you will have to choose the path in which you will take. But remember, no matter what path you take, the Lord Jesus and I will always be there with you. If you do get in a tight spot, just call out to the Lord and ask him to send me. I think you call Him #1! I will be at your side as fast as I can to help you. Now, can you remember that? Can you remember everything I have told you? Can you now? Can you?"

"I don't think I will every forget any of this. This is great, I've got my very own angel. Wow!"

"Evan, you must take this gift very seriously. Most of your problems will be solved in the Word of our Lord. Calling for me must be the last choice you have. However, Christ wants you to know that I am here for you, when you're right and when you're wrong. It is very important that you stay on the path of the Almighty God. You must fulfil your chosen path in life. There will also be times when our Christ will send me to guide you, when you don't know what to do."

"Okay, okay, I get the message. I will remember. Boy, wait until I tell Father about you!"

"Oh no, Evan, you can never tell anyone about me. I mean you can never tell anyone that you can actually see me. It is okay to tell them that your guardian angel helped you out a little, but never no never must you tell anyone that you can see or talk to me. However, you can say that God has granted you the power of sight. It is your Christmas present from the Lord this year. Merry Christmas Evan!"

"Sight? What is that?"

"Why, the gift to see me and others. This gift is the gift of the discernments of the spirits, one of your first out of many gifts in the beginning of your growth in the Holy Spirit. We will learn more as you grow in the knowledge of the Scriptures. Oh my, we do have our work cut out for us don't we? Don't ask why right now, we'll get into that later. For now, you must promise, Evan, never to tell. You must promise!"

Seeing that Jeffery was very upset at the fact that I might tell someone about him, I agreed.

"Don't worry Jeffery, if that is how #1 wants things to be, then that's the way it will be."

"Oh, thank you very much, Evan. You are a good boy, yes a good boy. Now, before I leave you, the Lord wants you to give your father a message for him. It is very important that your father doesn't know that you are giving him this message. Do you understand? Do you?"

"No, I don't really think so?"

"What I mean is the message has to be given to him as a question. Let me explain. The government is going to collect all the Old and New Testaments and distribute new Bibles that only have the Old Testament in it. There is something your father needs to do before it is too late. All you have to do, without him knowing that I have told you, is get the message to him in the form of a question and God will take care of the rest. Now do you understand? Do you?"

"I am very surprised, but I think I do. As strange as it sounds I really think I do! Yeah, sure! But I, well, I don't have a Christmas present for you."

"That's great. I am so pleased that you understand. It is going to be a pleasure working with you, Evan. By the way you will be all right here in the dark. The only thing in this alley is Razor, the alley cat, out for a bite to eat. He won't hurt you as long as you don't bother him. He lives here at the mission too. How about looking out for him, will you? Thanks. Oh yeah, Evan, I did get a Christmas present this Christmas from you."

"Yeah! Well what did I give you?"

"You, Evan. You are my friend now that you can see me. That is a rare gift. Yes, Evan, you are my Christmas present! And I am well pleased. MERRY CHRISTMAS EVAN! And always remember, God loves you, Evan. God loves you!"

With that he vanished as quickly as he appeared. The alley, which was all aglow while he was here, was now dark, gloomy, and cold again.

Bewildered at what just had happened, I started to drag the trash cans back onto the back docks. Wondering why Jeffery had to leave before helping get the trash cans back to the docks, then I remembered. He said not everything would always be easy. All of a sudden a white and grey cat ran right in front of me, stopped, and looked up at me.

"You must be Razor? Well it is nice to meet you. I guess we will be seeing a lot of each other from now on."

After I got the cans back in their proper places I went into the kitchen and got a bowl of milk and took it outside to Razor, who seemed to be waiting for me to come back. I set the bowl down and the ruffled haired cat came over and began to indulge himself in the comforting bowl of milk. I tried to pet him on the top of the head but he would not let me. I guess he wasn't sure of me yet.

"Well, have it your way, you little beggar."

I started on my way back inside, when not a moment too soon, "Where have you been, Son?"

"Well, Father, getting the trash cans to where they needed to be was little more than I bargained for, a little more trouble than I bargained for."

"We need to get all the lights turned out before ten o'clock or the police will be banging at our doors. Come along now, let's get to bed."

As soon as Father started to walk away I took the chance to ask him for a little of his time.

"Father, I have tried not to keep you from your duties or your routine, but I really need to ask you something that has been bothering me."

"Why, of course, Son. I'll tell you what. Let me get the rest of the lights out so that the hometown police will have a good night. You go ahead and get into bed, I'll be right back."

With that, I made my way to my room and got myself ready and into bed just as Father had asked me. It didn't take Father long to do his lawful duty and return back to my room.

"Now, Son, what can I do to help you?"

As Father was getting himself fixed on the edge of the bed, I put both my arms under my head and tried to figure out how I was going to come up with a question about the message from the Lord, to Father.

"Well, do you remember when you were telling me about our government making changes in our laws that concerned our Bible?"

"Yes, Son, I do."

"What is that all about? I think I am ready to listen now."

"Well, son, the government wants to take the New Testament away from the people of all the nations in the world. If the government can take the New Testament away from the people then the way of our freedom of choice will be gone. The New Testament is where freedom of choice comes from. It's all right there, the way of right living. If the government can do this then they can fully humble the human race to be controlled like cattle, with no values of their own. We as a human race will not care what the government will do to us or to our world. By doing away with the New Testament our world will be free to enter into a one world government. We Christians have to work as hard as we can up until this happens, to gather in the harvest for the Lord.

"So, Son, does that help you understand it better? I know there is a lot more I could try to explain, but I don't even know if I know how God's got it all planned out. Except, that with God all things are good, possible, and he will take care of us."

"Yeah, I think so. I'll study on it a little more and I'll let you know. I hope I didn't bother you by asking you about it, but I just didn't understand."

"Oh, Son, you can always come to me with anything you are concerned about, besides, this little conversation reminded me of something I have been wanting to do for a couple of days now. I think I will get to it first thing in the morning, after I get the crew up and running at the shipping dock. So see, it was good that we talked about it. Not just for you, but for me as well. Very well then, let's get to bed. Morning will come before long. Goodnight, Evan."

"Goodnight, Father."

So off to bed he went. I couldn't bring myself to tell Father that I didn't have the slightest idea what he was talking about, but thanks to Jeffery, Father got the message he was supposed to get. I hope?

I have to admit that the bed in my room felt really good. It had been a hard, hard day, but it had been a day of bewilderment for me as well as for all the people around me, whether they knew it or not.

I lay there wondering if their lives were as complicated as mine, and if they knew their chosen paths. As I lay there with my eyes getting heavier and heavier, I decided that I would give up trying to figure it out. It is time for me to let the night come and tomorrow take care of itself. I only had one last thing to do.

"Goodnight Mother and Magna. May God's blessings be with you always. Amen!"

CHAPTER ELEVEN

MAGNA

Morning seemed to come as soon as I got my eyes closed. The bed still felt cozy and warm. I think I could have slept all day. I turned over in the bed and fixed myself just like I wanted. I started to cuddle back to sleep but falling back off to sleep didn't seem to be in the Lord's plan for the day. There was something in the air that seemed to be keeping one eye open. Then I realized what it was. It was the wonderful smell of bacon, sausage, eggs and who knew what else. Boy was it time to get up. Yeah, I was as hungry as a bear.

Up out of the bed I came as fast as I could. After I got dressed I made my bed and put my clothes up where they belonged. I took one more look at my room to make sure I had not forgotten anything. It looked just fine so I hustled out of the bedroom door as fast as I could without actually running. Down the hall I went in a trot until I came to the chapel. Then I slowed down to a walk. Rounding the corner I entered the room with a hardy,

"Goooood Morrrning!"

Focusing my eyes on the table where I thought I would find everyone with their orange juice, coffee, and bacon. To my surprise there was no one there. All of a sudden this sunshiny voice came from the other side of the room from the kitchen.

"Eya! And a very hardy good morning to you too! I am afraid you will not find your mates inside on a morning like this. Everyone is out under the bamboo hut. Breakfast is being served outside on this fine beautiful morning. The rains last night brought the whole place alive. It pleases me to find you up and moving. I was just on my way in to collect you for the others. They are busy putting everything together and they asked me to come in and hurry you along to breakfast."

I didn't know what to say for I did not know this man. Well I guess he was a man. He was acting like a man but he didn't look a day older than maybe sixteen or seventeen. This fresh, sharp, tailored stranger looked like he was some kind of sea captain or something. Ever since Mother and I arrived here at the mission everything seemed as if we had gone back in time. No one talked or dressed the way they did back home where we were from.

"Well, good morning to you too. If it is not too much of a bother, can I ask who are you?"

"Oh how clumsy of me. Let me introduce myself. I am Adam Cross. I am your everyday variety neighbour-hood processing guide. As a matter of fact, I just put my boots on solid ground this morning, in from Homeland. It is my pleasure to make sure that everyone and everything gets into and out of Homeland safe and sound. So my new mate, if I have your permission,

I find you to be a mighty fine lassie indeed. I think you are just as beautiful as your Mam. I introduce myself to you, my dear lassie. Never fear Adam is here, at your service mademoiselle."

All the while he was bowing at the waist like I was a member of royalty.

"Well, hello to you too. My name is Magna Straut. Grandfather Straut is my grandfather. I am very glad to meet you, Adam Cross. You are a very funny looking man, and if I must say so, sir, you're not from around here, are you? You talk like Brimie, the paper boy back home. Are you from Australia too? Brimie was born there and that brogue of yours sounds like you shared the same backyard."

With a big grin and his fist on his hips he gave me a big,

"Eye, Lassie I am. I, too, am proud to know you Miss Magna, they said you would be a sharp one and that I should keep a sharp eye open, for you had a wit about you. Eye, they were right. So come, let's be off to breakfast. Surely you can feel the old bread basket rumbling a little this morning?

"Well, a matter of fact I can."

"Then we are in agreement. Come with me now! If we don't hurry along, the morning will be at our backs and the day will be half gone."

"Well by all means, let's get started. I'm ready to eat. I'm starving!"

So hand in hand he led me out to where Mother and the rest of the members of my new found family were all gathered. Yes, Adam was right. Everything was beautiful. What a wonderful place to start the day.   .

As Adam and I went out the back door, every smell in the world came rolling in my nose. The smell of last night's rain was so clean and fresh. Every flower in the gardens smelled as if their sweet perfume had been bottled up and suddenly poured out at the same time. The waterfall was beautifully flowing and the smell of honeysuckle was in the air as well. Roses were running up the poles of the bamboo hut and the morning sun was tender and sparkly. Not only did the nature smell good but the breakfast smelled wonderful! And was I hungry.

"Hello, and the top of the morning to you all!" Adam announced as we were walking up on the others.

"Well, good morning to you my little Magna and to you too Adam! Thank you brother Adam! Did you have a time getting her up?" Grandfather Straut yelled with his arms opened wide to take me into them, ready for a big good morning hug.

"Not at all Sir, I think she was already up and look-ing for the food, Sir."

"Did you sleep well?" Mother asked.

"Oh yes! I slept just fine. I think I am a little sore from our boat trip, but I would have slept right on if I had not smelled this wonderful food. Everything looks great! I'm starving!"

"Well, don't let us let it get cold." said Dr. Yo.

Breaking into the good mornings Della got her say in as usual," I was going to wake you early, but

Honorable Father said to let you sleep. He said another thirty minutes wouldn't hurt you at all, but next time you get up with the rest of us. There will be no babying around here. Everyone must pull their own load."

"I think that will be enough my Honorable Daughter. This morning Magna will be treated as a guest, but as soon as breakfast is over she will be on her way to a full recovery of her journey to us, and I'm sure ready and willing to carry her load upon her on shoulders by the time the ships are ready to depart for Homeland. "

Giving me a salty grin to let me know that we were still friends, Della bowed her head to her father and returned a warm and loving, "Of course she will, Honorable Father."

Dr. Yo looked around the table to see if everyone was in their place. As he was deciding that everyone was settled down and ready to eat, everyone just seemed to get quiet and looked at the head of the table, where now Dr. Yo was setting.

"Now, if everyone is ready, we will go to our Lord in thanks."

At that, we all bowed our heads and Dr. Yo gave grace over the meal and the day. He also gave thanks for Adam returning safely to the mission. He asked God to take care of us on our journey back to Homeland. What stood out the most for me was that he asked our Lord's blessings on all who had given up what was important to them so His Word would live on. That reminded me of Evan and Father.

It was a strange and painful feeling bubbling up inside of my heart. My eyes began to puddle with tears. I thought I had gotten past the tears. As I began to wipe the tears from my eyes with the back of my hand I couldn't help but look up to see if anyone else was reminded of anything or anyone like I was. As I looked around the table I could see that everyone had at least one tear running down their cheeks. Della and Mother both had their napkin up at their noses. As for me, I was stopping my tears and getting a good lick in on my nose with my sleeve at the same time.

Adam put his finger up to his face and softly wiped his one tear away. He was holding the rest back. You could tell by the quivering stiffness in his jaw.

Grandfather had tears slowly running down his face but instead of wiping them away he lifted his head proudly and held his shoulders back squarely. It seemed as though he was showing tribute with his tears. He reminded me of Father, I had seen him do the same thing many times before. I guess we pick up a lot of things from our parents that we don't think about.

Dray's voice clearly was swallowing his tears as he tried to finish the very powerful prayer from which we were to start our day.

I guess everyone had given up something or someone that was very important to them to carry on the Word of the Lord. As Dr. Yo gave a humble, "Amen", and the rest of the table gave their whispery, "Amens", to show their respect to the Lord, our new day had truly now begun.

While all this was going on I decided right then and there that I would make sure that I would always do my best to honor my parents and Evan for their sacrifices. It had not dawned on me that I too must have a sacrifice of my own. That fact would not be revealed unto me until much later on into my journey.

With that everyone composed themselves and began grabbing for the delicious   food spread out on the bamboo table in front of us. There were scrambled eggs, bacon, sausage, and toast made from French bread. At the other end of the table there was sliced pineapple, a bowl of peach halves, and the biggest and reddest strawberries I had ever seen. As a matter of fact, now that I think of it, everything seemed to be bigger and more beautiful than anywhere or anything I had ever seen before Mother and I arrived here. There were several pitchers of different juices and one of fresh milk. I didn't know about anyone else, but I was going to eat until I popped. This was one meal I wasn't about to miss. No sir-reee!

During the meal the men and Mother talked about the boats and all the supplies we would need for our journey. Then Grandfather said something strange that really got my attention.

"Now Adam, are you sure that the little one's pets have been carefully hoisted over the sea river dam and have been carefully placed on the other side of Lovestream?"

"Oh yes, Councilman Straut. The crew has been working on that all morning. Before I came up to the flat I made sure everyone was on their way just like you requested. I will leave you soon to make sure that we will soon be ready to depart on time."

I didn't understand anything that was going on. What pets? Surely he wasn't talking about Snow Cap and Fin Tale?

Then Adam continued. "There is only one thing, Sir. Fin Tale has a little one herself, and a newly acquired mate. We will have to bring them along, too, Sir. I ordered the crew to make sure her new family came along for the journey. I hope that was okay with you?"

"Of course my son, we never separate a family unless there is no other way, and we're not about to start now."

All at once everyone started to laugh. I still didn't know what was going on. So I just asked.

"What, Grandfather? What are you all talking about?"

"Why, Magna, you didn't think we were going to leave Snow Cap and Fin Tale behind, did you?"

"Well, Grandfather, I really didn't think that they would be able to come with us. How can they survive in fresh water? Don't they need to be in salt water?"

"Ho Magna, the river to Homeland is salt water. It passes all the way through. This is the only way into Homeland, but the salt water flows back into the sea through underground caverns fandom's under the base of the mountains at the other end of this valley. Our fresh water comes from the falls. We catch it and recycle it for our use. God provided this wonderful place just for us. No where in the world is there another place in the world like this, where fresh water and sea water run together in this special way."

Bursting out of my chair and giving Grandfather a big bear hug, and thanking him with every breath I took, I begin to cry again.

"Oh Grandfather, how can I ever thank you for not separating me and my friends?"

"Now, now, there are no thanks needed. If you must show your gratitude somehow, then listen closely. You try to honor all these gifts that have been unselfishly given to you and grow into not only a good Christian, but a strong and courageous Christian, and that will be thanks enough for me."

Now pressed tightly against my Grandfathers chest with his loving arms crushing me with love, I gave my word that I would always honor the ways of our Christian family, no matter what the cost.

"I promise, Grandfather! I Promise! No matter what the cost, I promise!"

"Well, let's hope the cost won't be too high. Now, you and Della go to the second beach head and watch as they get your friends on their way to Homeland."

Jumping out of her chair Della gave a hardy "Let's go Magna, you're going to love this."

So off together we ran to see Snow Cap and Fin Tale and their families on their way.

Giggling while running side by side, we took off in the direction of the upper end of the cliffs. There we came across an iron railing and steps which were strong and well built. They seemed to go off in a couple of different directions which led to different levels of the cliffs, the shore line and the sea river.

Looking down at the waters below me once again I couldn't believe my eyes. There was a dam made of what looked like tree trunks. At the crossing of the dam there was a bridge made of huge, flat stones. It wasn't overly big, but it was big enough. I guess didn't see the dam the night before because of the cloudy darkness. Or either I had my mind on the other end of Lovestream. Anyway, this was just the coolest sight to behold. I was really giving the dam, with its wide bridgeway, a really good over all look. I saw that it went all the way across to the falls on the other side. There wasn't anything here that didn't have a purpose. There wasn't anything that was not made by hand, or at least if it was made some other way, you sure couldn't tell it.

Hearing the splashing of water to my right, I saw Snow Cap and Fin Tail and their families safely swimming on the upper level of the deck of the river. They were just fine. Yes, I could tell by the way they were splashing around, happy and free. I saw almost ten or maybe twenty men, working steadily, loading not just one boat but three boats with all kinds of different boxes, barrels, and even livestock. Pigs, cows, two horses, several crates of chickens, and believe it or not, a baby elephant. My mouth flew open. He was so sweet! His little trunk was blowing sweet little sour notes because it didn't want to go aboard. The men were having a bit of a time getting it to go aboard. It was just one more thing I found wondrous about this new life of mine.

Della was already down on the dock where the boats were anchored. These boats were more like Father's shipping boats. Hey, you know, I'll bet that is how Father knows all about boats. Everywhere I looked, everyone I met, every new turn I took on my journey to Homeland reminded me of who and what I had left behind.

"Come on, you slow poke!" Della yelled, and with both hands she waved me down to hurry up and come on down to the dock's edge with her.

"I'm coming!" I yelled back as loud as I could.

So far, I had just begun to grow into the ways of Della. She seemed to always be right on queue with my mind. Whenever I was getting down, out of the blue, there would be Della. It was as if God had put her here to watch after me and keep me smiling.

Well, that's what Dr. Yo said. He said that we would become like sisters. Della was a mighty strong willed girl. Somehow I could see us knocking heads at some point. Della really liked to have things her own way. I find myself studying her a lot. Some times she reminds me of Evan, telling me what to do when he thinks I'm getting too clumsy. She is truly an amazing girl. However, she could never take Evan's place in my heart. Oh no! I could feel my heart filling up again.

All of a sudden my soul jerked me a little and I realized that I was talking to myself. Boy, do I need to get a move on before I get so depressed I would start to cry again. Out of the blue my heart talked backed to me.

"You and Della will be on your own a lot. Maybe you need someone to watch after you? Maybe you just have a lot of growing up to do? As far as Della, she is already on her way." Then, with a giggle in my heart I knew. "What's the matter with you, Magna? With Della by your side you're in good hands."

The closer I got to the side of the boat where Della was, I began to realize that the boats were pretty big. I guess they had to be to get all the supplies and other stuff that we were taking with us. There also had to be enough room for us, too. I certainly didn't know how long it would take for us to get to Homeland. I just figured we would need a place to sleep, and, well, you know, bathrooms and such. All this was going through my mind as I got closer and closer to the boats and the dock's edge. For a minute I was beginning to get nervous again.

The boats were not strange to me, Father had three just like them, but not quite so big. Yes, I was sure, the harder I looked the boats over and the nearer I got, I was sure of it. I would bet my next loose tooth that these boats were much bigger than Fathers. I guess they needed big ones out here in this wonderful wilderness, and if you are going to carry baby elephants around I guess you'd better have a big enough boat to put him on.

Yes, the boat's engine was up front at the bow. Then it tapered down for the smaller quarters. The rest of the boat was a huge flat bed for stacking and crating all the things that needed shipping. There were all kinds of heavy ropes and two cranes for heavy crates to be lifted from one place to another, wherever they needed to be stacked.

All this was familiar to me. And as always, all this made me think of Father and Evan. To think of them always brought tears to my eyes. When was this pain going to go away? I so desperately wanted to think of Father and Evan with only joy. I don't think that would ever happen, not for a long time. They were too dear and too far away.

Della's voice came out of the air, urging me to get back on track.

"What are you waiting on you...you...slow as a Japanese crawling shell snail?"

I flipped around, hunted up and down the boat getting madder and madder because I couldn't find her. I wanted to give her a hardy,

"STOP YELLING AT ME!" But I couldn't find her. Finally, I heard a healthy.

"LOOK UP HERE, YOU SILLY GIRL!"

"WHAT DID YOU CALL ME? Where are you? I can't find you!"

I was trying to get a good look at where Della was yelling at me from, so I could give her a good reply like,

"I CAN TAKE MY TIME IF I WANT TO!"

Again, Della came to my rescue. There, to my surprise, I spotted her, swinging back and forth on one of the largest ropes hanging from one of the sails next to the pigeon's lofts, one from the other. She looked like a monkey in a treeless jungle. I couldn't help but burst out laughing. I laughed so hard I almost fell right off the dock into Lovestream. I took a whirl around in a circle with my hands going apee. Suddenly I found myself landing half on the dock while the other half of me was over the edge of the railing of the walk board to one of the boats. Wow! That was a close one. After landing myself solid on my padded rump with my knees up to my chin, I looked up and watched my tough, sweet, and mischievous new friend having the time of her life. I sat there wondering if I would ever feel as happy as Della. She, too, had lost much to the Lord, but somehow she was tougher than me. I guess that's why God gave her to me as a friend. Della will always be there to see to it that I did my part and that I will have a ball doing it. Yes, God had truly blessed me. I wasn't mad anymore. How could you stay mad at Della? I stumbled back to my feet, brushed myself off, and gave Della a large wave to let her know I was all right.

"Hey you monkey, come down from there and show me the boats."

Swinging with one hand and waving back with the other, Della yelled back,

"Yes, Honorable sister! Right away! By the way, they aren't boats they are ships!"

Again my anger rose up in me, but not much, for I knew that. Father was always correcting me about the same thing. Della was right. Ships are what they are. I would have to remember, for she would never let me forget, I'm sure.

I kept looking up and watching my new friend and sister make her way down one of the never ending sail poles. Around and around the poles she came looking down every so often to give me another wave. Then, all of a sudden she looked up over my head and got this really serious look on her face. She began to quickly scuttle down the pole. It didn't take long for her to get over to where I was.

Looking at Della's face with such serious-ness I pulled her to my attention, and blurted out a bewildered,

"What?"

"Grandfather Straut and Honorable Father and the rest of the crew are on their way down. We must be ready to go."

"Well that is good isn't it?"

"Oh...oh yes, very much so. But...but I was not supposed to be on the sails up that high. Honorable Father has forbidden me to climb so high. If he saw me I will be in a lot of trouble."

"Ho-------. I see. Well maybe he didn't see you. Let's cross our fingers and pray."

Looking at Della with as much kindness as I could, I added a slight suggestion.

"I'll tell you what, I will tell your father that I asked you to climb higher and that you did it for me."

Della quickly turned to me with stern eyes and a moment of silence, and with much concern. Very tact-fully she became very straight faced. With much love for me she quickly responded to my suggestion. Putting her hand on my shoulder she softly began to explain.

"Oh, no. What kind of a friend would I be if I let you lie for me? That is not how we do things around here. If we make up our minds to do something and it is not right, we take our dues. No lying, Magna, no, not ever. Our Savior's Word says that a liar will not enter the kingdom of heaven, and I will not be the reason for you to dishonor the Word of our Savior. No way. No lying. Not even for me. We'll just see what happens."

"Oh Della, I'm sorry, I didn't mean…. Well, you know I wouldn't want you to do anything against you and your father, or the Lord." I was now hanging my head in shame, "Forgive me, I have a lot to learn don't I?"

"Well it is my understanding that we have a lifetime to learn about each other and a lifetime to figure out what our Savior wants us to learn. Honorable Father says the more we learn the more we think we know the truth. That is when we don't know anything at all. That there is always more to learn."

"Huh?"

"Don't try to figure it out now. You've got a lifetime."

"I have so much to learn, Della. Do you think I will ever learn all the Lord wants me to know?"

"As long as you have a willing heart for the truth, your heart will soak it up like a sponge. My mother told me that many times before she got sick and went to be with the Lord in Heaven, and my mother never told me anything that she couldn't back up with the Word of the Lord!"

"You are so much smarter than me, Della. I hope I will someday be smart like you. You also have some thing. Something I can't quite put my finger on."

"What do you mean there is something wrong with me?"

"No! I didn't mean there was something wrong with you. I said you have something. Something special, something very special, and gracious about you."

About that time Dr. Yo's voice came out of the air,

"It is called wisdom Magna."

Surprised, I opened my eyes wide as golf balls and slowly turned to see all the others standing there, all in a group.

"Ho, hello Dr. Yo. What? What did you say? Wisdom?"

"Yes Magna. For sure Della's wisdom is limited but she still has some."

"Maybe one day I will be as good and wise as Della."

"I hope so too, Magna, but you must remember there is a price for everything. The price for wisdom is very high, let's hope your wisdom comes slowly. If it comes too fast, you will lose your childhood. Stay a child as long as you can. For one day you will have to grow up and carry on with the Word of the Lord. So for now let's just enjoy."

Dr. Yo looked at me and Della with a big smile. He never said anything about Della and her deliberate mistake. As the others started to go aboard, Della and I looked at each other and gave each other a slight grin. As our grins open into wide opened smiles, we let the rest of our air ease out of our stiffened lungs where we had been holding our breath.

I let my body retreat back to a comfortable position.

"Boy, that was a close one. I think we got by with that one."

"Do you think so?"

"Well, don't you?"

"Remember my Honorable Father has quite a sly side to him too. The sun has not set on the day yet. And there is always tomorrow."

"I don't understand you sometimes, Della. If your Father had seen you, surely he would have said something right away and punished you, right?"

"Not necessarily. Father is like that sometimes. I remember the last time he caught me doing something I wasn't supposed to do. It was about a year ago. He had just gotten a load of fine sweet monkeys delivered. Right off he ordered me not to get around them until they had been cleared. I and my impatience got the best of me. I snuck out that very night and went into the cages with the monkeys and played with them.

"I was having what you call, the coolest time, letting them jump around on me and letting them pick at me. I lost track of time and all of a sudden I heard honorable Father calling for me. I climbed out of the cage and ran around to the front door and came in that way. I yelled at him to let him know that I was in the house. All he said was that he was glad that he found me and that it was time for bed. Of course I went on to bed without saying anything and found that I couldn't sleep very well. It bother me all night that I had disobeyed Father. He so much needs me to be good and honorable. It means a lot to him, you know.

So the next morning I got up and fixed him his favorite breakfast. I spent all day working as hard as I could on a lot of things that we had gotten behind on. I cleaned the chapel and mopped the whole mission hospital. Boy, was I tired. I was glad to see night fall. I was in the chapel giving my prayer of the day. Honorable Father came in and knelt down beside me. He took a candle, lit it, placed it on the altar and began to pray.

Of all things, he started to thank God that he had such a good and faithful daughter. He was talking to God about how proud of me he was. His prayer included how God had honored him with such a wonderful child to carry on our family's honor. All of a sudden I burst out and tried to interrupt Father, when he just spoke louder. Then he said it. I will never forget his words, "I want to thank you my most Honored Father God that Della has realized her disobedience to me. She has worked hard all day to see to it that when she is told not to get near the monkeys again that she will do whatever it takes to make sure that she will never disobey her poor, Honorable father again. Thank you, my Honored Father God, thank you for letting my Honorable daughter regain the wisdom she needs to obey." Right then and there he told God not to worry about ME. It was as if I wasn't even in the room.

Then he did the most wonderful thing of all. After his Amen, he turned to me and said,

"Your mother would be proud of you. Now come, give your Honorable Father a big hug and kiss so that we both can get to bed."

"You mean he knew all the time that you had snuck out to be with the monkeys?"

"Yes sister. When it comes to Honorable Father it is better to just do what is right. You see, he may know, he just doesn't say anything about it right away. We'll have to wait and see. Yes, we will just have to wait and see. Come along my new found sister. The adults will want to get us and the ships on our way to Homeland."

So off we ran to catch up with the adults and some of the other crew. The crew was already untying the ships from the docks. Everything was moving faster now and we were finally on our way.

Della and I ran back and forth on the deck of the ship and giggled at all the exciting things going on around us as the ships fell in line, one right after the other. We, of course, were in the lead ship. Yes, it was exciting! I could feel the excitement rushing through my veins. The water was splashing against the ships as the speed of the ships got stronger. Snow Cap and Fin Tale were happily flipping up and down in the water beside the ships as if they, too, knew we were on our way.

Then all of a sudden I began to quiver all over. It was as if my blood had turned to ice water. Stunned for just a moment, reality was beginning to dawn on me! I turned and leaned down on my knees. For the first time I realized that this was not a dream. This was real. Everything that had happen was real. Not a dream or something that could be explained away. This was real! There would be no turning back....

As I knelt there on my knees, with my head bent down, I began to pray. I wish I could tell you what I prayed for or even why I was praying. All I knew was that all of a sudden things were happening all too quickly. I don't think I had ever felt so alone in my life. Even with all the wonders going on around me. I felt hopelessly alone.

In my horrible loneliness I wanted to feel my father's arms around me, telling me that everything was going to be all right. But Father was not here. Father was far, far away. My eyes filled with tears. Father and Evan were all I could think of. Mother and I were so far away from them. Did they even know where we were? Yes, that's right, Father knows, but he's not here!

"Oh, Father!" my soul yelled. I wanted my father! The tears from my eyes just wouldn't stop.

All of a sudden I felt someone gently touch my shoulder. As I looked up from my tightly gripped slump of fear, I couldn't see clearly out of my eyes. I had to reach up and brush some the tears out of my eyes so I could see. Even though the sun was sparkling down on her face, I knew it was Mother.

"Magna, my dear, what is the matter? Are you ok? You are shaking as hard as a tree in a wind storm!"

"Oh Mother! I am afraid! I want Father with us! I'm afraid I'll never see Father and Evan ever again. Are they lost to us forever Mother? Are they?"

Mother knelt down beside of me and pulled me close to her.

"Come now, my little Magna. Don't be this way."

Mother and I got comfortable on our knees in each others arms. Mother rocked me back and forth, comforting me as much as she could. She pulled on my hair, fixing it out of my eyes where it was all mixed in with my face and my wet tears. After finding my face she spoke softly, "There you are, now."

She knew that would bring a smile to my face. Being safely cuddled in her arms helped my fear a lot more than I wanted to admit. I was supposed to be this real brave   girl, with a great mission at hand. Well, I can tell you that I didn't feel so brave. Maybe I would find out about that latter. Right now I was enjoying being wrapped in my mother's arms.

"Here now, tell me. What is causing you to be so afraid? Magna this is not like you at all. You were born with your father's courage, and my strong will. I have never known you to be this afraid of anything in your whole life. Now tell me if you can, where is this fear coming from?"

Turning myself to face Mother more squarely, I fixed myself with my knees up to my chin and as I looked over my knees, holding myself tightly, I tried to listen to my heart, for the words that would explain this strange feeling of fear.

"I'm not sure where this fear is coming from. You're right Mother, I have never been this afraid before, but I don't know if I know where this awful feeling is coming from. I don't know how to find the words to explain what I feel. Everyone has been so wonderfully kind, but, but, I don't know, Mother!" the tears ran heavier and heavier as I dropped my face back in my hands.

"Now, now! Just calm down and concentrate on your feelings. Sometime we're not sure where any of our feelings come from. I can tell you one thing, though. You've got your mind off the Word."

"What do you mean I have my mind off the Word?"

I was looking up at Mother now and trying to suck up my tears and talk at the same time.

"You mean the Holy Word?"

"Yes, I do Magna. If you need an answer to anything, you have been taught that the answer is in the Holy Word."

Pulling me closer to her Mother began to search her heart for an answer.

"Let's see. Let's see. Right now even I am having a hard time."

"You, Mother?"

"Why, of course dear, we all have times that we have to remind ourselves what the Holy Word is trying to tell us. And remember this is your fear not mine. Now let me see. Many, many times in the Holy Word there is a very short message that will explain all this away. In the Holy Books of Matthew and even Mark and on and on the Word simply says 'Oh ye of little faith.'"

"'Oh ye of little faith,' and what does that have to do with me being afraid?"

"Why, it means just everything dear! Everything! You must first find out what you are afraid of. Only then you can apply your faith to the problem."

Trying to get an idea where my fear was coming from, I untangled myself and sat up a little.

"While I know in my heart I miss Father and Evan something awful, and, well I guess I am afraid. I...I guess I am afraid that I will fail you and Father. I am afraid I won't be brave enough to become who you want me to become. That...well, that I will dishonor you both by not being able to do what I have been called to do. What ever that is? I sure don't know what I could ever do for our Savior that is so important?!"

"Oh Magna, none of us know whether we can do all that is required of us. Even Jesus' disciples were afraid, and they were grown men. Before you can overcome your fear you must first realize where fear comes from. In Matthew and in Mark of the Gospels, it tells us a story about fear.

"There was this one certain time that Jesus told his disciples to get in a ship and to go on before him to the other side of the sea and that he would take care of the huge multitude that had gathered to hear Him and be close to Him. His disciples did as they were told, just like you are doing now. They went away without Jesus. Well, you see, they had never been very far from Jesus before. You and I have never been that far from Father and Evan either, so I guess we know how the disciples were feeling about this time. After Jesus bid his disciples farewell, He did as he said and sent the multitude away and then went up into the mountain to pray by himself.

"As his disciples got about half way across the waters a storm came up. The ship was tossed about by the waves, for the winds were really bad and blowing against the ship something awful. Even though they were used to the seas they were getting pretty nervous about the storm. In the fourth watch of the night Jesus went unto them walking on the sea.

"Now when the disciples saw Him walking on the water of the sea, they were afraid. They cried out that Jesus was a ghost. Jesus of course called back to them,

'Be of good cheer, it is I, be not afraid.'

"Well Peter, one of the disciples, answered him and called his name and asked him to let him come to him on the waters. Of course Jesus told him to come right ahead. For a little while Peter could walk on the water toward Jesus, but he started to pay more attention to what was going on around him than keeping his eyes and his heart on Jesus. He started to watch the strong winds move the sea harder and harder under his feet. Well, with his eyes off of Jesus he began to sink and all of a sudden he cried out to the Lord to save him before it was too late. With much love Jesus immediately stretched forth His hand and caught him and helped him up. It was Jesus that helped Peter place his feet back on the top of the water. Do you know what Jesus said?"

"No Mother, what?"

"Jesus said, *'O thou of little faith, why do you doubt?'*

"Magna, you must never put faith in yourself. You must try to remember that we alone can not make anything happen right. No matter what we think of ourselves we must remember that that has nothing to do with what God truly knows about whom and what we are in our hearts. We don't know if we are strong enough to fight any battle which we are given. That is why Jesus fights our battles for us. It is our faith that sees us through this life and it is our faith that opens the door of heaven. Even to his own disciples Jesus had to say 'Ye of little faith.'

"You think I can't imagine how scared you must be right now. To leave almost everyone and everything you have ever known behind you. I know it has not been easy. I can tell you that I felt a lot like you do now when I left Homeland to spend my life with your father. I was not only scared, I felt lonely too. Even though your father was with me almost all the time, sometimes your father's love for me was not enough to stamp out the fear and the loneliness. But, my Savior's love was the secret. Together with the love of the Lord and the love of your father, with my growth in my faith, well, slowly but surely my fear became smaller and smaller until it was gone.

"What I am trying to tell you is that no matter what the responsibility of the day may bring, from dawn to dawn God is in control. The longer you walk with Christ you will learn that it is your lack of faith that causes you to fear. Just like Peter's faith became weak after he took his eyes and his heart off of Jesus. That was his human side as it is in all of us, and it's not going anywhere. As you grow, you will learn to walk in faith and you will learn what the meaning of fear is. Fear is nothing to be afraid of. You will someday learn to do what we call 'walking on water without fear,' just like Peter. You just wait and see. You will learn to walk the walk.

"Now come close to me. Let's be still for just a minute. For in the Word, Jesus spoke even more powerful words that I don't want you to ever forget. In the story I always imagined Jesus standing strongly and boldly as he was lifting His arms toward heaven and with His most wonderful strength demanding the storm into his will.

"Then Jesus spoke! *'Peace, be still!'*

"Then the sea and the wind calmed themselves and humbled their power to the Savior. Oh what a wonderful sight that must have been. You see, Magna, you cannot calm the storm within your soul, but our Lord Christ can."

"Oh Mother! That would have really been a sight to behold. So, if I am afraid of something it is because I am afraid of the failure of my faith. So that is where I make my mistake, for as you always say, 'Greater is he that is in me than he that is in the world.' Fear is from Satan not Christ."

"YES!"

"Unless my faith grows in my Savior, Jesus I will never be able to do anything because of my fear?"

"YES! Yes dear, that's right! Like I said, being afraid is only human. Being afraid and still letting Christ guide you in life and letting your faith take control of your fear is the walk of a Christian. You must always remember it is your lack of faith that places fear in your heart."

"Will I ever learn everything God wants me to know?"

"I doubt it, but you have a lifetime to try. You know all that the Lord asks of us is our best. Remember Magna, none of us ever know what the end of the day will bring. We can't see that far ahead. So just remember that you must first start the day before you can end it. It is like that with anything that we do for our Lord. Faith is the essence of things not yet seen. When we start something for Christ we ourselves have no idea where God is taking us until He gets finished."

"Oh Mother, you and the Lord are so good and patient with me."

"Well, the Lord and I are proud to have you on our side."

We gave each other a big hug. From now on I will just have to test my feet upon the waters. I'm going to walk the walk.

CHAPTER TWELVE

EVAN

I awoke early. It was still dark inside of the mission. I couldn't tell if the sun was up yet, for the mission was a really huge place and our newly assembled rooms were far away from the front windows. There were wooden shutters that covered the mission windows at night, and they never let much light in while they were folded closed. Everything was so still outside my door, I was sure I was the only one awake.

I lay awake for a long while until I just decided to get up. The small clock on the night stand had hands and little numbers that glowed in the dark and the clock plainly shown bright: 5:08.

Getting up early was slowly becoming a habit. After changing my clothes I quickly made my bed and grabbed my backpack. All of a sudden I heard rumblings coming from the side of the mission where the kitchen was.

I finally stuck my head out the door of my room. Sure enough there was a dim light shining through the small windows of the doors that lead to the kitchen.

As I passed my Father's newly built room I stopped and peeked through the curtain to see if Father was okay. I found him sleeping soundly.

Again, the rumbles from the kitchen got my attention. With my boots in hand, and creeping along in my socks, I continued to quietly sneak my way toward the bathrooms and the kitchen. I would stop in the bathroom and finish cleaning myself up for the day before I found out what was going on in the kitchen. I figured that was the least I could do. After my surprising meeting with my guardian angel Jeffery, I didn't want to meet anyone else in the dark with my shoes off, if you know what I mean. Ha ha. I couldn't help but laugh a little on the inside. All of the things that had been happening lately seemed like the highlights of a bad nightmare.

I reached the bathroom all right and the only thing I needed to do now was to just hurry up and get cleaned up for the day before I checked out the kitchen. It didn't take me long to complete the washing of my face and combing my hair, nor any of the other morning habits including the brushing of the old choppers. A little mouth wash I'm sure would be welcomed as well. In the men's bathroom there was an old wooden box with a padded lid on top. You could sit on it while changing your clothes. Inside of it is where you could find cleaning supplies for the bathroom. In one of the corners there were a couple of old school lockers. There you could find towels and washcloths. There were body soap and shampoos as well. There were razors and face soaps so the men could shave and clean themselves up a little as they passed through.

Around here at the mission I knew it would be different than at home. Here, the others and I had to think about everyone else's needs first and put our own needs to the side. For me it was a new way of thinking. The mission could get pretty busy, I'm sure. I never had to give up my life for others before, but I have heard Father tell stories about those who have. Here is the only place in town to find a little peace of mind. The most important thing to most people who come through here is a good bath, a good meal, a good sermon to give you the strength to face tomorrow, and last, a good night's sleep on the inside, off the streets where you didn't have to sleep with one eye open. And then sometimes that didn't even happen.

I studied myself in the mirror for a brief still moment. Looking at my face real close I was wondering if I looked any older? I sure felt older. Then I heard something that sounded like something fell. It startled me and I began to hurry up so I could check out what was going on. Checking out my hair one more time in the mirror, I rushed to the outside of the bathroom to discover that there was more life coming from the kitchen. As I slowly entered I couldn't see anyone. I could hear a real soft voice singing.

"Vvviiiccttttorrryy innnn Jesssus."

I started to sneak up on the voice. As I finally reached the end of the long stainless steel counter I popped around to find a startled Stacy turning quickly, and, now in total shock, dropped a big stainless steel cooking spatula to the floor.

"Oh, Evan! You scared me so. Oh…I couldn't even scream!"

While I was picking the spoon up off the floor and gently handing it back to its startled companion, I tried to apologize.

"IIIIImmmm ssssorrryyyeee! I thought…well… maybe you were an angel or something!"

"An angel?"

"Well, you know!"

"Yeah right! An angel? Maybe you should be glad I'm not! Do angels fry sausage?!? Well?"

Stacy was standing there looking ten years older than she was. After getting a good look at her she was pretty mad too. Even her face was red. She looked funny in her house coat, and her hair all twisted up in a towel. She looked like a bundled up teddy bear.

"I'm beginning to worry about you Evan Straut!"

"What, worried about meeeeee? Please don't worry about me. I'm just getting used to everything around here. What about you? You're awful young to be in here cooking at 5:00 in the morning?"

"Look here, Mr. Evan Straut," now waving her spatula like a weapon, "I may be young, but my dad has to have a good meal before he goes to work every day. You know, this food is not only for my dad, but for you and Brother Straut as well. There are a lot of things that have to be done before the day starts! Or don't you know anything about that?"

I found myself standing, wondering. For a little girl, she sure did know how to take care of not only herself but others as well. She must have really had it bad at sometime to never think of herself like this.

Realizing that I was taking too long to answer her, Stacy got even madder.

"What? Evan! What?"

"What! What do you mean 'What?'"

"You're staring at me!"

"Ohhhhhhhh, your hair is wet, and that towel is bigger than you are."

"Oh yeah, you think!!!!! It just so happens that I get up early every morning. I like to get me a good shower before all the others. It gives me a head start on the day. Not only that, I've got my clothes soaking in the utility sink. I'll be a mess until I get all of this out of the way, and I'm sure not going to get anything done standing here trying to figure out if you are okay or not!"

"Really, I don't care what you look like! Listen, I'm sorry I scared you. I'm already cleaned up for the day. Can I help you do anything?"

"Well, can you fry sausage?"

"Yeah, I guess I can? I really haven't had to do much sausage frying. I guess it's just like cooking outdoors. Father and I cook outside when we go fishing. Sure, why not?"

"Great! Let me cut the heat down and then you can watch the food while it cooks. Then I can finish up my clothes and get dressed for the day. Just stand here and let it slowly cook. I just put it on so I should have plenty of time to finish up my clothes and get dressed for the day. Then I'll get back to the breakfast. It won't take me long. The others won't be up for another 30 minutes or so."

Moving quickly but surely, Stacy went to finishing up her clothes. She went outside and hung them up on a line that ran across the back of the docks. After coming back in she took a look at the sausage.

"This is cooking too fast!"

She lowered the heat on the sausage. As she looked around the kitchen, she picked up a glass and grabbed the orange juice form the fridge. Pouring the orange juice, she began spouting orders again.

"Here! You take a glass of orange juice and I will go get cleaned up for the day. Don't touch anything. I'm not sure you know how to take care of yourself yet. You were right when you said you were just getting used to all of this. Now, remember, don't touch anything. Not one thing you don't know anything about. Just watch the sausage and don't let it burn. I've cut the heat down, so I'm sure you will be okay until I get back."

With that, she was off. I just stood there for what seemed to be forever. I began to be troubled within myself. There were all kinds of feelings going through me. I missed Mother. She was supposed to be here fixing my breakfast. Magna was supposed to be squeezing the oranges for breakfast, and Father was supposed to be standing in the kitchen teasing Mother about her cooking and giving her a kiss for being able to make the best coffee in town. I could feel that anger stirring up in me again. I walked out onto the docks to see the sun rising over the cliffs. I somehow can't get a handle on this terrible feeling in the pit of my stomach and the tightness of my chest as if my heart could burst out of my chest at anytime. How would I ever be able to get this under control?

Looking closer into the sunrise seemed to calm me and believe me, I like being calm instead of being angry.

I couldn't get Stacy out of my mind either. How young she was, but yet how old she acts. I began to wonder about myself as well. Where have I been? The world I'm used to is the world where kids are the kids. The adults take care of the kids. All of a sudden I realized that I had been pushed into a world where kids are taking care of themselves, and as far as what I've seen, their parents too. I guess you would call this new world a bit crazy and topsy turvy. It's like life as we know it has been erased and that we have been put in that bad nightmare I was talking about. Surely someday I will be able to understand what is going on, but where are all the parents? I'm just not sure if I know what has happened to everybody. Why must it be us, the children, who have to do it all and give up everything? I wondered way I was even thinking about all this anyway. All of this made me dizzy and kind of sick to my stomach. Boy, I needed to get a hold of myself or I wasn't going to be any good in helping anyone or helping with anything. Every time I get alone like this it seems as though I get into one of these moods. I guess it was better that I just stay busy and around a lot of people. That's the way Mother would handle it. About that time I heard someone call my name.

"EEEVVAAN!"

As I turned I saw Stacy standing with her head stuck out the huge screen door that led from the docks into the kitchen.

"Evan, if you are hungry, you need to come on in now and get some food in you. You'd better be glad I came back and checked on you and the sausage, or all you guys would have gotten for breakfast is eggs and toast. Dad and Brother Straut are already finishing up their breakfast. Hurry along now!"

"Oh man! The sausage!" One good smack on the forehead woke me up. I started to turn to go in when I had to stop and take one more look at the sun which was now climbing higher over the cliffs. I let Stacy know I heard her. "Yeah, right away, I'm coming!"

As I entered the kitchen I could see where Stacy had our plates already lined up along the shiny counter top. Father and Mr. Anderson were finished with breakfast and getting what was probably their last drink of coffee. Father was discussing how helpful Mr. Anderson had been since he and Stacy had arrived in town.

"Brother Anderson, without your help these past few weeks I would have never gotten the government food delivered on time. Not only that, Brother Anderson, in today's world it is hard to find someone you can trust, and someone who cares whether or not others are fed and taken care of. So when I say it's worth another dollar on the hour, I mean it's worth every dime to me just to have a brother whose heart is in the work of the Lord.

"And then there's Stacy. Look how she helps out around here. You've got quite a girl there. Why, she can almost run this place by herself. She does it without pay, too. All of us could never do enough to repay her."

"I just don't know what to say to you Brother Straut. It was hard going before Stacy and I got this far up the coast. Stacy said if we just followed the shore line that Christ and her mom would show us the way. I have to admit, I was about ready to give up when we made it this far. Stacy is my post upon the Rock, if you know what I mean. At first I was the one keeping her spirits up until I had one failure after another, then she started lifting me up. She told me to stay strong and the Lord would plant our feet on good ground. I think she got that from her mom and the Bible. Stacy! Tell Brother Straut that story you told me about good ground."

"Oh Dad, I don't know? I love that story but Brother Straut doesn't want to hear it. Anyway, I can't tell it like Mom told it." Stacy was now looking very withdrawn.

"Oh, go ahead Stacy. We've got a few minutes before we have to get out of here. Go ahead!"

"Well, like I said, I could never tell it as well as Mom, but I think it goes something like this."

She stood straight up with her hands behind her back. She looked like she was in school, about to recite the Pledge of Allegiant or something important like our Constitution, or some other great saying.

"The story begins in Matthew chapter 12. I'm sorry but I can't think of what verse, well, lets see? I think Jesus had been out doing his daily ministry for His Father. He had faced a few Pharisees and cast out some unclean sprit in a man. Jesus was also tired and walking through dry places, seeking rest, and finding none. Well, in the same day Jesus went out of the house and sat by the sea side. All of a sudden a great multitude was gathered around him. There were so many people about him he found refuge in a boat and sat upon it and drifted into the sea, just so the whole multitude could stand on the shore and be near him. He spoke many things unto them in parables, just so they could understand the wonderful meaning of His Holy Words. Then Jesus said...let's see, I want to say it just right. Let's see. Okay!

> *'Behold, a sower went forth to sow; and when he sowed, some seeds fell by the way side, and the fowls came and devoured them up. Some fell upon stony places, where they had not much earth: and forthwith they sprung up, because they had no deepness of earth. And when the sun was up, they were scorched; and because they had no root, they withered away. And some fell among thorns; and the thorns sprung up, and choked them. But other fell into good ground, and brought forth fruit, some an hundredfold (100%), some sixtyfold (60%), and some thirtyfold (30%).'*

"Jesus begged the multitude to listen and take heed of his words, for if they did, they would find and plant their feet where our Lord and Savior needed them, and there he would take care of them. Most of all, the story not only tells us of finding our good ground, but that we must plant as many seeds of faith along the way. Mind you, they must be good seeds to take root in one's heart. If we keep going, and keep trying, Christ will lead us to good ground. Then it is there we can plant our feet on the rock and stand grounded in the word of our Lord and Savior."

I was amazed at the passion with which Stacy told the story of our Lord. You could tell that she believed every word of her loving Bible story of faith. I was not able to speak, but Father was.

"My goodness Stacy, how beautifully you told that story of the Lord. If we all could know and feel the truth of that wonderful gospel story the way you do, how much better off we would all be. You are so right about that story. It not only tells of the good ground we are now standing on, it is true that it also tells us of the seeds we must sow while we are passing by. Maybe you can tell it to our guests one day at lunch. If you can tell it like you just did, I'm sure you will touch and encourage someone's heart."

"Oh my, Brother Straut, I don't know."

"Well, you think about it, okay?" With a slight pause of silence Father recaptured the duties of the day.

"Well that story has a lot of good tales in it and if we tried to tell them all we would be here all day. But I can tell why Stacy is your post upon your Rock. Stacy is every bit strong enough to lean on as long as both of you stand on the Rock of the Lord. Good job my man, good job."

"She never forgets to remind me of my promise to our Lord and her mom – not to ever give up. I will never break that promise, not ever.

"Before we get started for the day, please let me thank you for all you have done for Stacy and me. Finally finding true Christians that are doing something about what is going on, instead of grumbling about everything, was what Stacy and I both needed."

"Well, don't think anything about it. Just remember, I like to see our Lord at work, too. Sometimes in today's world we don't get to see God's wonderful blessings fulfil people's lives. Not here anyway. That's what makes this world a sad place. We'll just have to pray harder for this mixed up world of ours, right? In the meanwhile it's good to see God's blessings on good folk like you and Stacy."

Father put one hand on Brother Anderson's shoulder and shook the other hand in agreement.

"Right, Brother, and I'll say again, thank you. Now maybe I can buy Stacy some new clothes. She is growing up mighty fast."

Stacy was trying to stay polite and be quiet while the two men talked, but when she heard what her father said she burst in the conversation with triple wording.

"Really? Really Dad? New...new clothing! Oh Dad, do you think I could? Do you think I could get me some warmer boots? That's what I really need. Winter is going to be rough this year. Well, ssssooooo I hear."

Stacy was now realizing she needed to calm herself down. Her whole mood changed.

"Well Dad, I mean…I don't have to have new clothes. And my old boots are just fine. You don't worry about it anymore."

Then Stacy was calm again. She had a simple happiness about her too.

"I can get clothes at the second hand thrift store, or even right here. Miss Beverley has clothes in the back. We give them out all the time. She said I could have anything in the store room I wanted. So you just don't worry about me new clothes. I'm sure me and Miss Beverley can find all I need. You take that money and put it up for some other good reason. Someone else may need it worse than us. I'm sorry that I forgot about the people in need."

I was shocked at Stacy's response to her Dad. Why would he not want his own child to have what she needed before anyone else? Why would she give away her chance to get new boots for someone else to have what they needed? Man, I guess I had a lot of growing up to do. All the other adults and kids around here were always thinking of others' needs first, before their own.

Stacy's dad could tell that Stacy needed help getting herself out of her own twisted tongue. He could tell she was getting embarrassed at herself. Putting his hand on the top of her head he hurried the conversation along.

"Yeah now, let's don't really worry about that right now. Brother Straut and I have to get down to the docks so we can get that new shipment in for ourselves. The Mission Church can't feed the hungry on the crumbs we have here. The store room is looking a little empty. Come along Brother Straut, let's get to work."

All of a sudden Father realized I was at the plated breakfast leaning with my elbows on the counter top. I had been nibbling while they were talking. It seems as though Stacy and I both have been taught not to interrupt when adults were talking unless it was an emergency.

"Hey! Good morning, Son! How did your first night at the mission go? I hope you slept well on your new bed."

"Good morning Father, everything went fine. I slept okay."

"I see you have been up awhile. I hope you found everything you needed?"

He noticed the glances between Stacy and me.

"Of course you did! I'm sure Stacy helped you out with the things you weren't sure of. She has been a big help around here. Her coffee…well it's almost as good as your mother's."

Father quickly turned backed to Stacy.

"A matter a fact, sister Straut is the one who showed you how to make the coffee, isn't she Stacy?"

"Yes Sir! She sure did!"

"Let's see, Brother Anderson, I guess you and I had better get those front doors and shutters open. The morning is upon us. It's time for the day to begin. We'll have all kinds of men waiting on us at the docks. Sure has been hard lately, turning good men away. There has just not been enough work for all the people out of work. The crowd of unemployed men has been getting bigger and bigger every week, it seems like."

Dad was standing quietly now in the middle of the kitchen. That stillness was upon us again. As always Father broke the stillness.

"Before we go about the day let's pray."

Of course the ritual was to gather in a circle and hold hands in prayer. I laid my sausage down and went around the counter to where the others stood. Father took my hand and gave a sigh of relief. We bowed our heads and Father began.

"We call out to our Lord and Savior, Jesus Christ. Another day has come upon us to do your will in our lives. Lord, may we please you in all that we do. Bless this day and all of us who work hard to see our way home to you. You, Lord, and you alone, fix any mistakes we make and may we walk only for you, not for ourselves. We pray for all the families that have, and will sacrifice this day for you Lord. And if you are not too busy, Lord, could you peek in on Mother and Magna. Evan and I would surely thank you, Lord. We love you, Lord. May this day be yours and only yours. Amen."

With the Amen in place we all scrambled around in our own directions. Stacy went for an apron to clean the kitchen.

"You two men go on! I'll get the front opened up for the day."

Stacy's dad smiled and patted her on the back. "That's my girl."

Father and Mr. Anderson grabbed a bagged lunch off the cart against the wall in the kitchen. There must have been a couple hundred. They were made up the night before by a few of the visitors who spent the night. That much I did know. I had been here helping mop the mission one night when Father had asked a few to help. It was okay to pack them at night, for the only thing that they put in them was fruit and packaged pastries. It was never quite enough but at least it was something to pass out when supplies got short.

Sometimes they were bagged up and passed around the neighborhood. Father would get some of the visitors to help pass them out at night. I remember him coming home one night, earlier than he should have. I remember Mother saying how surprised she was that he and the men got through so quickly. I remember Father telling her that they had to call it a night. They had run out of bags and there were more people out that night than usual. Some of the clans got tangled up in the same area and he had to break up a fight over some of the portions of food. I remember them going out on the back porch together, and all the while Mother was patting Father on the back, telling him that he shouldn't worry. As they walked out on the porch the last thing I heard was something about how only God can make things better.

Getting my mind back on what was going on now I realized I didn't have a direction to go. Hurrying myself along, I saw Father and Brother Anderson making their way out the back screen door. I yelled at Father.

"Father, wait! Wait up a minute! What do I do today?"

Father just stood there with his mouth open and looking back and forth from me to Brother Anderson. Finally he spoke.

"Let's see now. What do we do with you today? I am afraid you need to stay in school son. Wait a minute! Stacy! Doesn't Miss Beverley teach half days on Tuesdays and Thursdays?"

"Yes Sir! That's right! She works over in the other county at the veteran's hospital on Tuesdays and Thursday afternoons. If the county lines are passing comers and goers quickly she will be there until 6:00 tonight."

"Thanks Stacy!"

"No sweat brother Straut."

"Well then Brother Anderson, why don't we take Evan with us today. We'll need all the help we can get at the docks. Although I'm afraid there will be a lot of men waiting on us at the docks today. There are so many of them out of work. Of course Evan, you will not get paid for your work. I can't work you for wages and ask a man with a family to feed to work for less or nothing at all. And with Christmas right around the corner, well, you understand, don't you, Son? Our Lord provides all we need. If you don't mind working hard and letting your wages go to the Lord then sure, grab a lunch bag, and come on with us."

Father was smiling and patting me on the shoulder as he was giving me my instruction. I turned and gave a hardy "Yes." when all of a sudden I was standing face to face with Stacy. There she was; one hand on her hip and one hand stretched out with one lunch bag ready to go.

"I'll tell Miss Beverley where you are today. I'll also get your homework assignment for tomorrow."

"Thanks, Stacy!"

"No sweat! We're working for the same Boss, you know?"

"We are? Who's that? Oh…you mean my father. Yeah, I guess we are at that."

"Boy, one minute I think you're getting smart, then you say something dumb. No Evan, not your Father! Jesus, Evan! Jesus! Even I know your mother would have a fit if you forgot that. I know mine would. Evan you've got to get your mind on what counts around here or you will never become what is expected of you. I can see I've got my work cut out for me."

I was now hanging my head about as low as it would go, "Oh…yeah."

Then I heard Father blowing the truck horn. My humbleness didn't last long. I turned with excitement and happily yelled back at Stacy.

"Have patience with me Stacy! I'm new around here! You keep me straight! Got to go! Bye!"

I ran outside toward the truck. Brother Anderson was telling me to hop in the back. As I hopped in and drop seated in the back against the cab of the truck, I looked back at the mission as we drove off. There I saw Stacy looking out the back kitchen door, and for a split second she reminded me of Mother standing at the front door of our old home waving good-bye to me as I left for school. Again, Stacy reminded me of how much I needed to grow up. That I needed to think about what it was the Savior wanted me to do with my life. Oh! It almost makes me mad again. I'm not sure I would ever know what Jesus wants of me. But, I guess at least I could try to find out.

The other kids seem to know what they are doing, even the ones that didn't claim to be saved or anywhere close to it. At least they knew what was expected of them. They know how to get food for their families and even take care of everyone in their different cliques. Man, this world seemed so divided. It also seemed so strange with all the kids taking care of everyone and everything. I wonder where all the parents were? I can't seem to get that question out of my head.

As Father drove toward the sea, the Three Ridges glazed in the morning sun like cut diamonds in the sky. I had to take my arm and cover my eyes from the glare. Then I remembered! Mother and Magna were some-where on the other side of those mountains. Again, the pain of not having them with me was almost too much to bear. Every time I thought of them my heart would fill up and tighten my chest as though it were about to burst. I was so lonesome with out them. I wonder if I will ever see them again. I know that I am not the only kid who has had to do without family. But I'm not used to my family being separated from each other. We used to be a family. I don't know how other kids get through the pain. The other kids were making it without their whole family, but look what they have to do to survive. They are making it, but they walk alone. To walk this lonesome walk without # 1 on your side has to be awful for them. Maybe they do let #1 help out sometimes. They do show up on Sundays and since they have been doing it longer than I have, I guess the best way to get through it is to let # 1 call the shots.

As Father's old, long bed truck made its way through our small fishing town I watched our sleepy little town come to life. Although times were bad the town tried to decorate the town up the best they could for the Christmas holidays. I waved at Brime, the mail man, as we passed the post office. Officer Washington was raising the blinds at the little block police department.

Our little town here at Three Ridges was a very small fishing town with one of everything. One really nice hotel and restaurant, one library, one Catholic Church, one Baptist church, one Mission and one retail grocery store with a line of small shops that use to take care of all the tourist coming and going. Of course, there were the government offices. Our most important town hall, jail and post office, and of course, there was the gas station and the shipping yards. The homes lined up in all their proper blocks, all in a line. Then, of course, there were the beach houses like our home.

We are only about 300 miles from Alaska by boat. This small town will never hold all the homeless people that were fleeing from the states around us. They were all lined up along the streets. Some still asleep and some starting their fires in the garbage cans the city gave permission for them to use to keep warm. Father was right; our world here in the United States was changing and changing fast.

All of a sudden the truck came to a screeching stop. It stopped so fast I bashed my head against the back of the cab of the truck. "Man that hurt!" I stood up as soon as I could and rubbing my head at the same time. I heard Father yelling at me,

"I mean it Evan, don't you even think about getting out of this truck. You stay put!"

Still rubbing my head, "Hey, what's going on!"

Father and Mr. Anderson went running to the pier. There, a huge crowd of men were arguing with each other.

Father started yelling out someone's name as he and Mr. Anderson tried to push their way though the angry mob.

"Hey! Stonie! Stonie! Stop! Stonie don't! Wait!"

Father got lost in the middle of the crowd. I couldn't see him or Mr. Anderson. I wanted to get down out of the truck and be with my Father, but I didn't want to disobey him either. I couldn't see a thing so I climbed up on top of the cab of the truck.

This was a lot better. I could see everything from up here. I saw Father trying to hold back this guy from another guy. About that time some other guy jumped Brother Anderson from behind. As quick as a wink he flipped the man around and threw the man on the ground. He was standing over that man when another guy started to grab for Father. Brother Anderson just went into motion and kicked that man in the stomach, and that sent him flying into some of the other men and made them fall down as they tried to catch that guy.

"WOW! Mr. Anderson could sure do some kind of fighting."

About that time a hole in the middle of the crowd started to appear and now I could hear Father and the others.

"Calm down all of you! This is no way to be treating each other. And what is the matter with you, Stonie? This is not like you. I am ashamed of you!"

Stonie was a big guy with dark skin and light brown hair pulled back in a ponytail. I had never seen him before. He must be someone new around here, but Father seemed to know him well.

"I'm sorry, Brother Straut. I guess I let my temper get the best of me."

"I guess you did! Now why are you men arguing and fighting like this?"

"Hey, because of what these kids are saying about you. They're saying that you are not going to be able to work us anymore. They say you sold out to the government. I told them you wouldn't do that. If you don't work us what can we do to provide for our families?"

"What kids, Stonie?"

Stonie started to look around the dock where everyone was gathered. Hurrying to point in the right direction, he swung his arm around and pointed his finger straight as an arrow.

"That's one of the kids sitting over there!"

I was trying to see who Stonie was talking about. Finally I saw a smaller figure clear the other men and step into the clearing. Oh no, it's Tommy! I couldn't believe it! I jumped down from the truck and went running over to my Father's side.

Surprised to see me, Father was repeating his request of me.

"I thought I told you to stay in the truck Evan!"

"I know, Father, but you may need me."

I was now up close and eye to eye with Tommy.

"I don't want you to get hurt, Son."

About that time Tommy spoke up.

"Oh no, we wouldn't want the preacher boy to get hurt, would we now!"

I anchored my feet square and let Tommy know I was ready for anything he wanted to dish out.

"Don't worry, I won't get hurt, and if I do I won't be the only one. Will I, Tommy?"

All of a sudden the smile on Tommy's face faded away.

Father's voice came from the thick silence from behind where Tommy and I now stood.

"Just remember to get out of the way if anything else starts up!" Looking at Tommy, Father got down to business. "Now young man, what is this all about?"

Stonie didn't give Tommy time to speak.

"He says you don't have jobs for us anymore, unless we sign up with the government."

"What?"

Father was now addressing Tommy again.

"Come here, Son. What are you talking about?"

"Come on, I'll show you. It is nailed on the outside of the dock post. Come on, I'll show you! "

We all started following Tommy over to the lead ship. Father had three.

"See! Read it for yourself Preacher! I told you—I told you!"

Father, Mr. Anderson, Stonie and I all tried to read it all at the same time. Finally, after stumbling over each other, Stonie pulled the paper from the post and with one glance got permission from Father to read it aloud. It went like this:

"NOTICE"
TO ALL CONCERNED:

THE GOVERNMENT HAS SEIZED TWO OF THE CHRISTIAN MISSION CENTER SHIPS TO BE USED FOR GOVERNMENT USE ONLY. THE CITY AND STATE COUNSEL FEEL THAT ONE SHIP IS PLENTY TO ACCOMODATE THE NEED OF THE CHRISTIAN MISSION CENTER.

THE TWO LEAD SHIPS WILL BE MONITORED BY SGT. TEALLY FROM THE U.S. MILITARY CORPS, STATIONED AT CITY HALL. ONLY MILITARY PERSONNEL WILL BE ALLOWED TO USE OR BE ON DECK AT ANYTIME.

ANYONE FOUND DISOBEYING THESE ORDERS WILL BE ARRESTED AND POSSIBLY IMPRISONED.

WITH SINCERE REGRET,
THE UNITED STATES GOVERNMENT

The men around us were murmuring amongst themselves. Father was standing there lifeless.

"Father!—Father! What does this mean? I thought the ships were your property?"

"They were, as of three weeks ago. I had to sell them so I could get support for you, Mother, Magna and the Mission, but they promised me that I could continue to use the ships! I have it in writing! I don't know what is going on, but I'm going to find out. I promise!"

Father turned to the crowd and began his apologies.

"Look, I promise I will get to the bottom of this. Just calm down and go back home to your families."

The crowd was really shuffling around now. Stonie came out from the middle of them with his hands waving in the air.

"How will we feed our families?"

Father, who was much shorter than Stonie, put his hand on Stone's shoulder and tried to assure him and the others that everything was going to be all right. His tiny voice tried it's best to top the shouts of the others.

"Listen! Listen! I know everything looks bad right now, but fighting among ourselves is not going to feed our families. I promise all your families will eat today. Bring your families to the Mission Center tonight if you have no food. You and your families will find everything you need there. All I ask is if you have food for a couple of days, use up all you have then come to the Mission. We will do all we can to help."

Holding his hand out to Stonie to seal the promise, Stonie took Father's hand.

"Well, okay? But you won't be able to feed us forever on promises!"

"You know, Stonie, you're right. I can't, but if it is God's will, he can. God promised He would never leave nor forsake us, and I believe that with all my heart, Stonie. God loves you very much. He does not want you and your family to suffer at the hands of others. That is not God's plan for you. Times are hard for everyone in the whole country. We all must try to be patient."

They stood their ground with each other and then Stonie's big grin came on his face. Stonie started helping Father move the others along their way.

Brother Anderson was helping Father move the crowd along too. He and Stonie got the others off with pats on the backs and handshakes of promises. I could tell Father was glad for the extra help.

After the last of the men went off, some alone, most within their small binding groups, Father, me, and Mr. Anderson came back together, looking at each other with grateful glances that brought us together in agreement. We were sure glad that was over, and that God didn't let anyone get hurt. For sure it would have been us. Except Mr. Anderson, that is.

"Hey, Brother Anderson, where did you learn to fight like that?"

"Oh, Evan, that's right you don't know do you? I spent five years in the Special Forces of the armed services when I was just out of high school."

He was trying to walk away but I wouldn't let him.

"Wait a minute, I want to hear more about this."

"That was years ago. I try not to think about it unless I just have to. It is better to solve your problems without a fight, but sometimes the bad guys just won't let you walk away. Your father would just let them walk all over him. Here lately I feel like the Lord led me this way just so I could be your Father's body guard."

He was now standing by Father's side. Brother Anderson had this grateful look on his face as if it was an honor to be standing side to side with him.

"Yes, and I have to admit that I have felt that way too. If Brother Anderson had not been around on quite a few occasions I feel I might not be walking around right now. I think just the size of his muscles helped change some of their minds."

The way Father was rubbing the back of his neck made me realize just how bad things were getting.

"Really, Father? Is it getting that bad?"

"Yes, Son, I'm afraid it is. What you saw today was really not so bad. Lately it has been much, much worse at times."

I was just now seeing what my father and some of the others were doing to continue their work for God on a daily basis. Actually, their lives were the price of a good day's work, a good, long day. I turned with my head hanging in shame. The shame of still being such a big baby about everything. I seemed to be doing the shame deal a lot lately. How could I have been so selfish and caught up in my life that I didn't even know that my father and mother were putting up their lives every day for what they believed was the call on their lives? All I could do was just stand there in shame. Then I heard a voice. I though I was going batty, when I realized it was the voice of Jeffery, my guardian angel. His voice was inside my head and wouldn't stop.

"Ask Brother Anderson to teach you what he knows. The Lord has sent him to protect your father, but he has been sent to teach you the arts of a soldier. You must ask. You must. Our Lord expects it. Our Lord expects it. Go now. Go now! Ask! Ask!"

I slung my self around and ran up to Brother Anderson and with a squeaky voice I asked, "Brother Anderson?"

"Yes, Evan?"

"Can you teach me to fight like you?"

"Well, Evan. I don't know about that, Son."

He was looking cautiously at my father.

"I don't know what to say? You will have to ask your father about that."

Father didn't say anything. He just listened.

When Father didn't reply, Brother Anderson continued.

"Evan, I don't want to disappoint you but there is a real huge responsibility to know what I know. Fighting my way means that once you use it you will always be forced to use it again. It is a big responsibility to know that you can kill another human being with just one blow. You will have to talk it over with your father."

I knew I was on the right track because Jeffery told me to ask. I walked over to Father and looked at him straight on, and asked. "Well, Father, what do you think?" Can Brother Anderson teach me how to fight?"

"Come here, Son."

Father sat down on a wooden crate and just looked at me without saying a word. After thinking about it for a minute or so, I knew in my heart what my Father needed to hear from me.

"Father, you sent Mother and Magna away. You are praying that they take care of each other, right? "

"Yes, Son, I pray for that every waking hour, every minute of the day."

"Well, it is getting bad here and our world is changing. You were right. It's time. You and I both are going to need to know how to take care of each other, in a lot of different ways."

Now I was not able to stand in one spot while I explained to Father my plan. I didn't want to worry Father, but I was afraid of a lot of things. If Tommy and the other gangs found out that I wasn't as tough as I acted, I would be in big trouble. I was also afraid that something would happen to Father, for he was all I had left, now, here with me.

"Father, you're not the only one who has to stand up to these people. I have my own standing up to do. Oh, I don't want to hurt anyone. And I know that taking another man's life is something that I would have to live with for the rest of my life. Can't I have your heart and Brother Anderson's knowledge of protection?"

Father just sat there with his head down and studied what he had just heard come from his young son, who didn't sound like a little boy anymore. As always, just as the silence was getting thicker than fog, Father's voice cracked the silence.

"Evan. You're right!"

"What?"

"You're right! The world is getting a lot tougher than it used to be. Brother Anderson has a good heart as well as a good fist, and his feet seem to know just what to do when they are needed as well. You are also right. Goodness and kindness we both can teach you. Brother Anderson can teach you other things that I never learned. All I ask, Son, is that you never let your anger get in the way of what the Lord would have you first,1- think through thoroughly about what needs to be done.

2- Never let your anger start a fight because you can never win a fight when you are angry.

3- And remember that Brother Anderson's way is not always the right way. The fist is always the last resort to settle what can be settled no other way."

"Your Father is right, Evan. It would be an honor to show you how to protect you and your loved ones, but not at the cost of your soul. It is always better to do it the Lord's way first. My way is when the Devil leaves you no other way out."

"I know, I know, Father. I really do. Father, I love you. Just in the last few days I have seen and learned more about what has been going on in the world around me. And there is a big responsibility of what it takes for those who love the Lord and their families, and what we all must endure every day for His sake. I just want to be the best I can be, so I can be here for my family and for the Lord. That's all I want. Believe me, Father, I don't want to be a hero. I just want to be the best

Christian I can be. I'll be fifteen in February. I think I need to get started, don't you? "

Father was stunned to see me, for the second time, on my way to manhood. He saw Jesus bring me to my knees and cause all kind of emotions to wave up inside of me when Mother and Magna left us. I think he knew when I got up off my knees from that loss in my life that I had changed in some way, but I don't think he was ready for this big of a change. I don't even know if I could explain the change that had come over me. Did this mean I was growing up? Or was it the actual experience that for the first time I saw Father physically attacked? I think I was realizing that I didn't need to make Father's life more difficult, or maybe I finally realized I loved someone besides myself. I guess none of us would know until I am put to the test.

"Well, Brother Anderson, do you think you are up to the challenge you are about to face? I think you have you first student. As a matter of fact, I think our Lord has chosen your path. Do you think you are up to it? "

"If it is what you want for him, I would be honored to make him the best soldier for the Lord I can. With you engraving the armor of God in his heart and me preparing the body, our Lord will have quite a soldier on his battlefield."

Mr. Anderson stood very quiet and hung his head, as if to humble himself before us and God. Lifting his head slowly and coming to an eye to eye contact with Father, he spoke firmly and proudly.

"I would be honored to train soldiers for the Savior."

"Well then, my brother, when you have time could you please show my son some of that fancy foot work of yours?"

"Well, he seems to have the right heart for it."

My father put both hands on my shoulders and pulled me close to him in his arms and held me tight.

"Yes, that he does."

"Oh thank you, Father! Thank you! I won't let you down." I was glad to return my Father's love hug. It was an honor.

Coming over to my side, Mr. Anderson bent down and looked me firmly in the eye. I knew he was going to mean business when he stared.

"Don't ever think that knowing how to take care of yourself in a fight, is enough. You may know how, but the Lord does the taking care of. Without our Savior, nothing is possible. Only through Him are all things possible. When I started out as a young, unsaved Christian, I thought it was me with all the power of life and death in my hands. Then, as I sat beside my wife's grave with all this knowledge and strength, I couldn't bring her back. I learned that day that God is the one with the power over life and death. I am the instrument by which God uses. This knowledge will not do you any good at all when God decides to take control. This way you must let God lead you into the wisdom of when and when not to use it. The toughest thing you will have to do is to die, so you can live."

"You're right Brother Anderson. Son, God didn't say easy. He just said possible. Always remember, to die is to live."

Brother Anderson turned quickly and ran his hand through his hair.

"Doggone it, Brother Straut, there you go again. I know what that means to a military solder but how does that fit into the walk of a Christian? What does that mean anyway? I've heard you say that a thousand times. When I think of the martial arts, I understand, but when you apply it to the Lord's work I'm confused. I know there may come a time that you will lay your life down for your country, but I guess you will have to explain this one."

"Dear Brother, it is really very simple. We must die to the world. It is not a physical death but a spiritual re-birth. The world would have us do everything the way everyone else does it. We must die away from or lay down the old us and pick up the new us. We must put things of the world away and yet still live in the world. To follow the way of the world is the way to destruction. The way of the Lord means life everlasting. So if you 'die' or put away the ways of the world, you live everlasting with the Lord. It's simple. It really isn't any different from what a soldier does on the battle field for his country. We Christians have a battlefield of our own. But it is not only against flesh and blood it is also against principalities and the supernatural. In our world today with its spiritual and moral decline, not only do we put the armour of the Lord on, we also have to be armed with a sure military battle plan. Our men, young and old, are giving their lives everyday on the battle-field overseas and here at home, too, for the right that we may worship our Lord and Savior. They also fight the fight for the America as we know it, to return. I am afraid the old ways will never return again. The world doesn't know it but the Lamb of God, our Lord and Savior Jesus Christ, is on his way to collect His children (His army) and then come to set up his kingdom. But before the final battle can be victorious we must win our battles here and now."

"Oh yeah...I see! It's always simple, the way you explain it Brother Straut."

"Yeah, it may be simple to understand, Brother Anderson, but not simple to live. For a long time when a soldier went to war he knew who his enemy was. In our army today you can't tell who our enemy is. They don't wear uniforms so you can see and know who they are. The enemy today hides itself. It hides in the darkness until all of a sudden it strikes. So now the wars of the world and the wars of the Spirit are all wrapped up in one neat little package. The only trouble we have is that the majority of the human race doesn't believe it, or doesn't want to believe it."

"Yes, Brother Straut, I understand. To become very good at the arts you must remove yourself in your mind from anything that might distract you from what you are attacking. At that moment it is just you and the next step, while all the time you are keeping up with everything around you with everything moving in slow motion. You kind of remove yourself from the destruction while yet you are still in it. Fighting your way through it? Yeah...yeah, I get it! I get it now! It really is a raging war until the end."

While I was beginning to grab hold of a little under-standing into this new life of mine, Father all the while was still kneeling down in front of me, looking straight at me with sternness I had never seen in my Father's face before. The only human thing I could see were the diamond shaped tears which were now running from where they were puddled in his eyes.

"Well, as I said, it is simple to understand Brother Anderson, but still very hard to live up to!"

"Evan, your father is right. I will teach you what I know, only know this! You must always try it God's way first."

Going back and forth from father to Brother Anderson, my eyes watching their sternness, it almost made me give up on the idea, but inside my head and my heart I kept on hearing Jeffery's voice saying, "It's God's will! It's God's will!"

"I will! I will! I promise!"

Brother Anderson was now looking very stern at me over Father's shoulders. Father was just stooped there in front of me, looking at me.

"Listen, Evan, I mean it! Just because you know how, your best defense will be, the less you use it, the less you will have to prove yourself. It would be bet-ter to be a good and humble man like your Father, and live by the word alone. Once you use your arts to stand up for the Lord there will be no turning back to just the ways of your father. There will always be someone ready to prove that they are better and stronger than you. The meeker you try to be, the simpler your life will be. The gift I am about give you could be one of the most important gifts God could give you. It could also be the biggest mistake of your life. If you can't outdo the Devil with it, if and only if, you use it only as a total last resort. It will never be important to prove yourself to any man, but you must always prove yourself to Christ!"

I stood there, taking in every word from what was now two of the most important people in my life. I now realized very well that my boyhood days were coming to a very sudden end. I thought that had already happened, but I know now that to become a man is a day by day job. I could tell that this was going to be one of those big decisions I would have to make on my own.

Then I heard my Mother's voice from within my heart. "Someday you will take care of us, Evan. That's why you have to learn all this nerdy stuff."

I looked up into my father's eyes and without a blink and only a few tears Mother had the answer to all the doubts for all three of us.

"Father, Mother always told me that knowledge of any kind is a gift, as long as our Lord is the author of that knowledge. I'm not trying to be a big shot or anything like that, I just know in my heart that this is the right thing to do. If I get the big head or something even worse like that, just give me a big swift kick in the dark side and light up my way again. You may not know it, Father, but we are Word Walkers. That means we have to make our walk count."

It took about thirty seconds and then Father laughed out loud.

"Word Walkers, ay? Okay Evan, I'll hold you to that!"

Father was now on his feet again and was giving orders.

"Brother Anderson! You can drop me off at the Court House and let me see if I can find out what's going on around here. Then you and Evan can get at least one truckload of food back to the mission. Come along, let us fill up the truck and get this day moving. I have something very special to see to today for the Lord. It will have to be done before the sun is down for the day. Come, the Lord's work won't get done this way."

"Father?"

"Yes, Son."

"Did we win today?"

"Any day that we decrease and see to it that Christ increases, we win. Always remember, Evan, when we win our battle for the day, Jesus wins. Still Evan, remember, Jesus won the war along time ago. Where the problem comes in is, the world and the Devil just don't want to believe it. So therefore we have to fight. Everyday the battle rages on."

With that we were off doing what we had started. As I thought to myself, I couldn't help but think, it never fails lately that the Devil always gets in the way of what needs to be done. Boy, I wonder? Has it always been this way? When you wake up, the battle starts and there is no rest until bedtime, and sometimes not even then. I don't know if I'm up to my newly chosen path the Lord has outlined in His plan for me, but all I can do, I guess, is try. I have learned one thing since all this has started. I really had the walk of a Christian all wrong. Thank God I found out before it's too late.

CHAPTER THIRTEEN

MAGNA

Our journey to Homeland was almost over. We had been sailing leisurely for two days. Della and I had plenty to keep us busy. We helped feed the animals everyday. The baby elephant was on our ship. Della and I would take turns feeding the huge, hairy bundle of joy. There was also a couple of sheep, three baby lambs, and a few monkeys. The little elephant was taken from his mother so we had to bottle feed him about four times a day. Feeding the rest was a snap.

We also helped out in the kitchen. Although it was work, it was the fun kind of work. Della would make sure of that. She would sing or make games up to make our time in the kitchen go by faster. Sometimes she would even toss me the dishes as we were drying and putting them away. She had really learned how to enjoy her life here with her father.

Most of all we enjoyed watching Snow Cap and Fin Tale. Their families stayed along side the ships in the water. We also found us our own special place at the top of the highest decking. There we would lay in the sun, talk, laugh, and sing, but most of the time we just took naps. At night we would lay and look up into the sky and count the stars.

All through our journey I would watch the mountains cliffs as we slowly passed. They stood like giant walls which held enormous carving etched in the side of the walls. Every so often you could see symbols or figures that led the way on either side of us. If you talked too loud your voice would echo. Along the very bottom of the water's edge was what I guess you would call a tiny road. Although it didn't look big enough to be a road except maybe for walking on. When I asked about it, Della told me that it was the burro route. It was where you could use horses and mules to carry small supplies or even take a trip back and forth from the hospital into Homeland.

She added that her father many times had been called back into Homeland by the Call of the Horn, and, as always, Della began to patiently explain.

There are always two men standing at the entrance of Homeland with huge bone-like horns. They stand on top of the giant pillars on either side of the entrance. The pillars are shaped like giant angels with their arms and wings stretched out to form the gate that keeps Homeland safe. This lets the colony know when the supply ships are coming. They can also call for help if something is wrong, or if someone is in trouble. That's when you can call for the doctor. She explained how many nights her father would hear his Call of the Horn and off he would go to save the day. The horns made different sound for different reasons. She tried to sound out the many different tunes the horns would make, but the harder she tried the sillier she sounded, and again Della and I engaged in rolling laughter. She sounded a lot like our little elephant friend and his shrill tones of discomfort.

Della and I were taking one of our getaway times after a long day of chores, when I heard Mother calling for us.

"MAG-NA! MAGNA!"

I ran to the edge of the decking. Looking down over the railing I saw Mother looking up and shielding her eyes from the sun. It was straight overhead now and Mother was looking right into it.

"Yes, Mother! Here we are!"

"Come along now. We must prepare ourselves for Entry."

"Entry!"

I turned to Della and with confusion all over my face I asked still another silly question.

"Entry? What is that?"

Della, now with her hands on her hips and shaking her head back and forth, walked over to the railing and answered Mother right off.

"Sister Straut, we'll be right down!"

Della and Mother gave each other kind of a wave to one another and then she returned back to my training.

"Boy, Honorable sister, they didn't tell you anything did they? I guess they wouldn't. We don't talk about it really, outside of Homeland."

Then Della turned and started to walk away. I started to follow her with a hefty step, trying to keep up with her.

"Hey, where are you going?"

"We've got to get our things ready for Entry."

"Della? Hey Della!"

Della turned quickly in a half circle. She planted her feet steadfast and firm in place, then, with one sharp look and one breath of air she gave her reply, but not before she flipped herself around again.

"What?"

"What is Entry?"

"Homeland, Magna! Homeland! We're almost home!"

Della was wearing a big smile on her face as she turned to look back at me.

"You are about to see the most wonderful place on earth. Just think, Magna, it's our home."

All of a sudden I realized that our journey was almost over. I knew we were on our way to Homeland but I think I was just now realizing the wonderment of it all. Or have I? Or by entering Homeland, did it mean that I was just beginning my journey? Questions, questions, too many questions!

"Are we really there? Really?"

"Sure as the sun came up this morning. Come on now. Everyone will be waiting."

So off we started down the steps that led back down to the bottom deck. There Mother was waiting for us at the bottom of the steps.

"Well, girls, are you excited? I am!"

Mother was rubbing her hands together, smiling from ear to ear and was acting like a little girl.

"It's been a long time since I've been home. Della? Is it still as beautiful as always?

"Well I don't know what it was like when you left, but as far as I'm concerned it's got to be the next best thing to Heaven."

"Oh, of course it is! I can't wait for the night to fall!"

Mother couldn't be still. She turned to walk back to the others when all of a sudden she turned and grabbed Della by the arms.

"Oh Della, are the Hosts as wondrous as they have always been! Listen at me, I'm asking too many questions."

"I haven't see them but once in my lifetime, Sister Straut, but wondrous? Well...lets say, well, maybe even glorious!"

"I know, I know. They are glorious, I know! I can't wait!"

About that time Mother pulled me close to her and gave me a great big hug.

"Oh, we are the most blessed people on the face of the earth. You will see tonight just how blessed. The Hosts will come to lead us unto Entry tonight. They come under the cover of the lost tip of the Aurora."

"The WHAT?"

"Oh, Magna, you will see. I don't want to spoil it for you. The first time you enter with the Host is something that only you can experience for yourself. Right, Della?"

"Yes Magna. You will just have to see and feel it for yourself. A wise mother would never take the moment of new sight from her daughter. And a wise mother you have been graced with."

They stood there smiling at each other. There was something between them, something silent, almost spiritual. I could feel the closeness between them. The wonderful thing that was about to happen, that they knew and I didn't, pulled them closer together with arms stretched out and hands clenched together. They were almost giggly, and yet brought together in a strong unexplainable belonging to each other. I, too, wanted to be a part of this wonderful thing that was about to happen.

"Mother, oh Mother! Tell me! Tell me! "

"Oh no, not me Magna! I'm not going to spoil the most wondrous surprise of your life!"

"Is it going to be that wonderful, Mother?"

"Yes Magna, oh yes child!"

All of a sudden Grandfather's voice was heard over our giggles of excitement.

"You now, come along here! We must get ready! Come ladies. Come ladies. Now come along!"

We all three clenched hands and off to the bow of the ship we went where Grandfather was standing with Dr. Yo.

"Come along now, you women mustn't delay. We've got to get ready before nightfall."

As we sculled up to where the men were, we were out of breath and giggling.

"Oh, Grandfather, are we there? Are we almost at Homeland?"

"Yes my child, we are."

As he was bending down and picking me up into his strong, assuring arms I heard him giggle with a burst of happiness.

"Oh yes! Oh yes indeed! My child, you are going to see one of the most beautiful sights on earth. Nowhere else on earth can you see what you are about to see to-night, as we are welcomed into Entry into Homeland."

"Really Grandfather, really? I can hardly wait."

Dr. Yo answered this time.

"Today, Magna, you will grow in wisdom and knowledge of the wonders of the closest thing to heaven on this earth. You will see what others could only dream of seeing."

"It almost sounds too true to be real. For just ordinary people like us, to be granted such a blessing, and I don't even know just how blessed I am yet."

Then Mother touched my knee, for I was still in Grandfather's arms, and that put me well above mother's head.

"I promise, Magna! You will completely fall in love with the wonderment of all the miracles of Homeland."

Grandfather gave me a great big hug and put me safely back on the deck of the ship.

"We must wait for the first signs of the fall of darkness, and then the lost tip of the Aurora will come. Then the whole symphony of the Heavenly Host will come. It won't be long now!"

I walked over to the tip of the huge deck and clinched my hands tightly on the railing. I had this feeling I couldn't explain. This feeling was something growing inside of me. What was it? It didn't quite feel like excitement. Could it be fear? What was the strange thing that was happening to me as I stood there with my eyes toward heaven, waiting for the sun to go down?

I turned and went with Mother and Della to clean myself up. We women made sure we were packed up and ready to go. We slowly gathered ourselves on the top deck, one at a time.

I guess it wouldn't be long now. The sun started dropping lower and lower behind the mountainside. No, not long at all. I just wish the trembling in my legs would go away so I could at least be standing on my own two feet when this most wonderful thing in my life came about. Oh well! I'm learning that sometimes in the world of Christianity that waiting and patience is the best game in town, and always worth the wait.

All of a sudden Brother Adam called out to Grandfather from the ship behind us.

"Are you all ready up there, mates?"

Grandfather turned right around and returned the response that Brother Adam was waiting for.

"Right away here, Adam. We're all willing and ready."

Grandfather took a glance back my way. He seemed to know that I had all kinds of feelings pouring out over the side of the ship. Giving Brother Adam a hearty wave to continue slowly on, Grandfather walked back over by my side. His large, gentle touch on my head was so tender and loving. I loved that feeling of safety and love. He handled himself just like Father. I am so lucky to have Grandfather. He's not Father, but he's the best next thing, in my book.

"Magna, what is this? You should be happy and excited. Why has your heart saddened so?"

"I was just wishing that Evan and Father could be here with us. Why can't they be here? Why do we have to be separated?"

"Your Father has a job to do for the Lord. If your father was doing what he wanted he would be here with you and your mother. Your father has laid his life down for the Lord. Someday you will understand. It takes time and patience to realize that your life is not your own, and yet it's your life you have secured."

"You know, Grandfather, I will never forget Father's last words.

"To Live Is To Die."

"What does that mean? I've thought about that a lot?"

"Your father, not unlike the rest of us, we live our lives according to the Gospels of our Lord and Savior Jesus Christ. The saying 'to live is to die' comes from the gospel of John. In John it tells a story of certain Greeks among Christ and some of the disciples. The Greeks wanted to see Jesus. Now Philip and Andrew came and told Jesus. Well, all I know is, to their request, Jesus answered them saying, 'The hour is come that the Son of Man should be glorified or honored. Verily, Verily, I say unto you. Except a corn of wheat or a seed fall into the ground and die, it abideth alone,

But if it die, it bringth forth much fruit.' Also, in II Timothy the 2nd chapter the Lord tells us to 'shew thy self approved unto God, a workman that needeth not be ashamed, rightly dividing the word of truth.' Now, back in John the 12th Chapter the Lord states, 'He that loveth his life shall lose it, and he that hateth his life in this world shall keep it unto life eternal.'

"I know this is kind of hard to understand. Jesus was always telling stories so that he could help his children to understand what would make their lives much easier to live and fulfil their hopes and dreams. It's not that you die in the physical body, it's that you die spiritually from the world and the ways of the world. To carry the Word of our Lord to the world, you must learn to walk in the world, but you must die to the world and what it stands for. For Satan walks to and fro in the world seeking whom he may destroy. In John 12:26 the Lord continues to tell us, 'If any man serve me, let him follow me, and where I am, there shall also my servant be, if any man serve me, him will my Father honor.' So therefore, to live is to die.

"In II Timothy the 2nd chapter it says, 'It is a faithful saying: for if we be dead with him we shall also live with him.' It is very important that we strive to live. Live the fullest life we can, so that we can be used of the Lord to lead his children home.

"As we go into Homeland we will be closer among the supernatural spirits of the Living God than any humans on earth. We are truly blessed to have been chosen. I know in my heart that this is a lot to understand at this point in your life, but it is the path in life your father and mother have chosen to take. We hope you will, or have already chosen to take the same path in life. But remember, Magna, no one can choose your path. God has already put your life into motion. The Lord knows where you will plant your feet in the end. He has known you since the beginning of time. The adventure for you is whether you take the right road home. Our Lord will never force you to walk a Christian life. For most Christian walks in life are not easy. The easy way of the world is to walk the world's way. It takes courage and a whole lot of heart to walk your way, *to*, *for*, and *with* Jesus. Thanks to Jesus we don't have to worry about salvation, but remember, you and all the rest of us will stand before God some day. Well, just think about what I've said, someday you will understand."

Grandfather rubbed the top of my head and turned to start his responsibilities to get ready for the coming attraction. I turned quickly and called out to him.

"Grandfather!"

Grandfather stopped and turned to look at me with a swift twist of his head.

I ran to his side and pulled on his clothes to bring him down to my level.

"Grandfather, don't worry. I understand. I don't know why I understand, but I do. I will honor my father and mother. I will follow their ways, and I already love their Lord, for he is my Lord too. If my Lord, or my father and mother would not approve, then I won't do it. I will work hard to become the best Christian I can be. I don't know if I will do it right, but I am going to give it all I've got to make them all proud of me. I promise."

Tears started to drip from Grandfather's eyes. I reached up and wiped them gently away.

"Don't cry Grandfather!"

"Oh my little chosen one, you make me so proud. The Lord has already planted so much wisdom within your soul and heart. I have a feeling you will be teaching me instead of me teaching you."

"Oh, no, Grandfather, you are the one the Lord has placed by my side. I am sure I am to learn all you can teach. I promise I won't leave until I can learn no more from you."

"So be it, my little Magna, so be it. That is probably just what the Lord has planned."

The sun was beginning to set behind us. We were all facing forward to the inside of the long straight of Lovestream that led our way home. Everyone was so quiet. The only thing we could hear was the current of the waves against the sides of the ship, but as far as anything that breathed, whether it was animal or human, I don't think any sound or movement could be heard. It felt like time had stopped and that everyone and everything was standing around like one of those dummies in a store window. Even the baby elephant had hushed his squeaky bellows.

Darkness came on quickly. Everyone was still waiting, breathless and still. I was sure that we were about to hear an explosion or something. I continued to look around and gather in every site when all of a sudden

Grandfather slowly bent down to my ear and softly whispered.

"Magna! Look!"

Grandfather was pointing up at the sky. I tried very hard to look just where his finger was firmly stating the exact spot. Blinking my eyes so I could focus better, I thought I saw tiny streaks of light. Then I saw very long streaks of lights in every color in the rainbow. They were far away, up high in the sky, and would suddenly flash off and on. They never quite got across the tip of the mountain tops, but they were still beautiful.

"What are they Grandfather?"

"It's the tip of the Aurora! It comes this far across, then stops here, only once a year. Can you see the lights? Look closer Magna. Look closer. Real close."

"Where, Grandfather! Where! "

"There, Magna, right under the tip of the lights, can you see them?"

"See them? See Who?"

"The Host! The Heavenly Host!"

Clearly hearing the excitement in Grandfather's voice, my heart was beating to the wonderment of what in the world Grandfather was taking about. I found myself looking back and forth from the heavens to the look on Grandfather's face.

"The Host?"

"The angels have come to welcome us to Homeland, Magna!"

"The angels?"

As I looked closer I began to see little specks of lights high in the sky. The closer they got, the bigger they became. Then all of a sudden, the golden lights were flashing around us everywhere. There were three large, golden lights that just stayed in a straight course in front of us. The lights from them were so bright I had to cover my eyes every so often to keep the glare from blinding me.

Mother and Della were laughing, yelling, and waving hellos at them.

"Hello! Hellooooo!"

Grandfather and Dr. Yo were just standing proud, as if something important was happening. As far as me, I was still pulling my head up and down shielding the lights from my eyes, wondering why all the others weren't having the same problem I was having. As my head was down on the railing for one of its glare fixes, Grandfather called my name and gently touched me on my shoulder.

"Magna! Magna, we have company! You need to look up now and focus your heart."

I slowly pulled my head up and began to look into the light that now engulfed the darkness. The darkness around us had turned into the sparkle of golden splendor. Grandfather told me to focus my heart, but all I could do was hold my hand up over my eyes and try to focus my eyes. Blinking and blinking, the glare finally came to view. I couldn't believe my eyes or the joy of my heart. Grandfather was right. There were three of the most beautiful angels just hanging in the air, right over my head. Out of all the beauty I had seen since Mother and I arrived here with Grandfather there were no words that could describe the wonderment of this magnificent sight now in front of me.

These wondrous new heavenly beings were almost transparent. Their flowing gowns glowed like a white fiery mist. Around their heads were lights that glowed as bright as sunlight. There were two lady angels and one man angel. The strong male angel was the angel in the middle. The beautiful lady angels were on either side of him. Not only these three glorious beings hung in front of me, but also all around them were little angels that looked like children. They hung high above them, moving in all directions, stopping every so often to look around in every direction. It almost seemed as though they were on duty as watchmen. The adult heavenly host seemed to be listening to all the little ones as they whispered to them. You couldn't hear what they were saying for there was music in the air as if a thousand soft voices were singing. You could hear those voices and the words being sung.

"Praise ye the Lord. Our Savior comes. Put on your garments of praise and praise the Lamb, the Son. Praise the Lord, for our Savior comes. You must put your armor on, and sing the battle song. "Praise the Lord, for soon he will appear. Praise the Lord and have no fear. Praise ye the Lord, Our Savior comes! HALLELUJAH! HALLELUJAH!"

The song and the music rang throughout the massive canon with its high walls. The song echoed over and over again. Even though it was loud and vociferous it was the sweetest song I had ever heard. And it touched my heart so, until tears filled my eyes. The song somehow humbled my soul. You would just have to be here. How can you find words to explain something like this?

The very handsome, strong, male angel in the middle suddenly gave me a wave and swung around out of place and one of the lady angels changed places with him. Now she hung over the ship in the middle. She had long, black hair as long as the gown she was wearing. Her hair and gown flowed like waves in the ocean. Then she raised one hand up slowly and graciously and the music and the singing stopped. All the angels small and great stopped right in front of us. The angel in the middle started coming forward, over the tip of the ship and kind of stood in midair over us.

All of a sudden Grandfather came over to the tip of the bow of the ship. He gave a humble bow to the beautiful lady and then came over to me and picked me up. All the while Grandfather was telling me not to be afraid. He took me over to where the lady was waiting. Grandfather, being strong as he was, lifted me up high in the air. I was beginning to feel pretty nervous about this time, when all of a sudden the lady angel came closer to me and bent down, softly touching my nose with her finger tip. It felt like the tip of my nose sparked. It felt like a gentle electric charge skipped across my nose. It tingled, and I giggled. She straightened herself up and went back to her appointed position in the line up with the heavenly host. After a short, silent pause there was a voice as sweet as any to be heard, and as loud as if she were using a speaker phone as she spoke.

"Grandfather Straut! Praise to our Lord that you have returned to us unharmed."

"Thank you, my Lady Carmel. It is good to be home."

"So, our new chosen one's soul is as pure as you have said."

"Yes, my Lady, she is. We are blessed."

All of a sudden as Grandfather was putting me down on the deck, Lady Carmel spoke to me.

"Hello, my little one. So, we finally meet, little Magna. Our Lord knows and loves you very much. Our Lord has sent you to us, to prepare your way."

"Thank you very much, Miss Angel."

At that response she laughed.

"You may call me Lady Carmel. I and the Lord have always been with you, but my main job is the keeper to the doorway to Homeland. Off and on I have been checking into your place in life. It has been a while since I saw you last. And before you ask, no you didn't even know we were there. But we have always been with you. It is my job to know every soul on earth. Only those of a pure heart can enter Homeland. As long as the love of our Lord is within you, you may come in and out of Homeland when the call comes to you."

I was confused, and of course I just had to ask, "And if you do not have a pure heart?"

"Grandfather Straut, she is indeed wise beyond her years. Let's see! Listen, little one, those without a pure heart cannot find their way on any road they travel, or any journey they attempt to encounter. They are blinded to the love it takes to walk and enter in."

"You mean, everyone doesn't love?"

"Yes, Magna, everyone loves. It just makes a difference what you love the most. To enter Homeland you must love our Lord most of all. Even with all our short comings, it's the love of our Lord and Savior Jesus Christ that holds the key to the door to Homeland. But it is not important to understand everything now. It is only important to have the tiny seed of faith to a pure heart. You, my Little Magna, indeed have that."

"If you mean, do I love Jesus, the answer to that is easy. Yes ma'am! I'm a Christian."

"Well then, my little chosen one, that's all you need right now. Our Lord has a lot of plans for your life. Now, shall we continue into Homeland?"

"Oh yes, yes please!"

With that, Lady Carmel raised her hand and the music and singing began again, as beautiful as before. The ship started moving slowly forward and the angels turned their brilliant glory around and started leading us into Homeland.

I could now see the truly giant gates that looked like angels' wings. There were two men on either side blowing huge horns that went all the way down to the ground. There were people across the stone ledge that went as far as the giant angels that stood at the gates. One lady seemed very excited the way she was running and waving. Grandfather was following her on her vigorous endeavour and waving all the while.

As the gates opened wider and wider I could see inside. Although it was dark, I could see lights coming from what seemed like all the homes. Over to the right, high on the mountain cliffs, I saw what I though looked liked ancient ruins.

Oh my gosh! Homeland is another world all to it-self. It's hidden from the rest of the world. How am I going to be able to become part of this magnificent place? I began backing up slowly from the railing of the bow of the ship. How am I going to know what lies ahead in there? Surely nothing on earth could be as miraculous as this. As I stood there, I realized how much the Lord Jesus was blessing me, but in a way that scared me. There was something that kept going over and over in my heart. Something my mother and father were always saying. I could hear it as loud as the horns playing their welcoming, "To whom much is given much is required. To whom much is given much is required."

Oh my goodness, what in the world would our Lord expect of me in return for this wonderful privilege of grace He is about to bless me with? I could not imag-ine me being worthy of this blessing. As I watched and felt the magnificence of Entry with half of its earthy love bubbling up inside of me yet its heavenly an-cient beauty of power overseeing with all its strength, I prayed, "Oh God, help me! What if I fail you? Oh, my Lord Christ Jesus, please, is it possible for me to be what you need for me to be? I know now that I am truly in the hands of your will, Lord. What is the world com-ing to if you are allowing us, your Little Ones, to see and encounter such miracles as these? Truly your coming, Lord Jesus, must be close. Make me worthy, Lord, make me worthy. Help me, Lord, to truly learn to live by and honor the meaning of my father's last words, 'to live is to die.' Please make my life count. And let me and my family's sacrifice, stand the test of love, just as you and your Son have sacrificed, and loved us, since the beginning. Help the world die within us and the You Lord grow, live and thrive within."

WORD WALKERS

HOMELAND

THE LAST GENERATION

This fictional adventure is a futuristic eye opener into the parabolic supernatural truth of the salvational decline of our world. Magna and Evan Straut, brother and sister, find themselves now separated and forced into their own life changing journey where they will spend their first Christmas apart and find the truth about themselves and their chosen path for Christ.

Being only children, can they become strong and obedient soldiers for the cause of protecting the Holy Scriptures from a deteriorating world, where government freedom, terrorism, war, disease, hunger, and moral and spiritual world decline is now taking over their world? Just how many souls can they reach, before it is too late?

Just children, can they learn the true biblical faith meaning of a true Word Walker? "To Live IS To Die?" Only God knows what lies ahead for them.